This Beautiful Place

For Pierre + Danalee,
Enjoy the book!
Best,
Ann E Post

This Beautiful Place

Tankred Dorst

with Ursula Ehler

Translated from the German
by Anne Posten

Hanging Loose Press
Brooklyn, New York

Hanging Loose thanks the Literature Program of the New York State Council on the Arts for a grant in support of the publication of this book.

www.hangingloosepress.com

Printed in the United States of America
10 9 8 7 6 5 4 3 2 1

Cover art: *Jacob's Ladder* by William Blake © The Trustees of the British Museum

Cover design: Marie Carter

Acknowledgment: An excerpt from *This Beautiful Place* first appeared in *Stonecutter Journal*.

Library of Congress Cataloging-in-Publication Data available on request.
ISBN: 978-1-934909-29-4

The *Loose Translations* Prize

In an era of increasing interest in global communities, can there ever be enough literature in translation? Certainly there is a shortage in the United States, known for its lack; and known, too, for its narrow attitude towards foreign languages. However, while it is true that our publishing houses do not bring out enough work from other nations, it is not true that Americans are monolithically monolingual or narrow-minded. Not in 2012. In a recent New York Times article, a writer asserts that most polls fail to take into account varying degrees of fluency--as opposed to fluent--which could include employees who learn some Spanish or Chinese for their work, soldiers back from the Middle East with "some competency in Arabic, Pashto or Dari," third-generation offspring who explore their roots, spouses and partners who wish to "pick up the language of a loved-one's family," and so on. ("Are We Really Monolingual?" by Michael Erard) True, we are not on par with other nations, but we are also not as xenophobic or arrogant as in decades past.

On our campus at Queens College, The City University of New York, there are 129 languages spoken. Our graduate and undergraduates benefit from an extraordinary cross-cultural community. Although reflective of exceptional diversity, such a figure also provides a vision into what this millennium holds in store: more linguistic exchange and greater interaction between previously autonomous communities. Meantime, our new MFA Program in Creative Writing & Literary Translation is producing students and alumnae/ni whose work often comes from languages and literary traditions quite dissimilar from our own. We believe that their translations deserve to be in print.

Towards this end, I thought to approach the independent press that gave me my first break. Hanging Loose Press has been publishing work since 1966 and the editors are as much friends and family as they are literary cohorts. Increasing the number of translations they've published struck me as a potentially valuable move. I asked two dear writer/translators, Susan Bernofsky and Roger Sedarat, to join me and propose that HLP host an award that would result in publication. Specifically, we three as an advisory board would forward three manuscripts from our students and alum submissions; the editorial board would then select one manuscript for publication. They loved the idea. The series name, Loose Translations, speaks for our collaborative mission to introduce voices new to English through translators able to foreground the extraordinary writing with which they work with great craft and attention to the original language. The goal of this new partnership is to publish innovative work that will emphasize the importance of something that often really does get "lost in translation": the world's diversity of cultures and the people who create and foster them.

This first book is certainly a cause for celebration!

Kimiko Hahn
Queens College, The City University of New York

ELEVEN O'CLOCK IN THE MORNING. He sits on top of some empty beer crates inside his apartment door, which is propped slightly ajar. He waits. Bella, his old mutt, is next to him. He waits for his food, waits for the *Zivi* to perform his civic service for the day, to spring up the stairs and hand him a green Styrofoam box with his food in it.

—Till, is that you?

It's not Till with the food, it's that unshaven guy from the fifth floor who never says hello. Irritated, Schlichmann shoves the door closed with his cane. No one cares about him, everyone just runs past him in their sneakers, no one ever stops for a moment and asks: How's it going, Herr Schlichmann, as he wheezes laboriously up the stairs. Bella's always with him. She's as slow-bodied as he is, but she always manages to drag herself up the stairs right behind him. Those goddamn sneakers! You don't even hear them coming, then they've dashed past you and disappeared! If someone were to speak to him, his answer would be: It's going well! and he would step casually aside, feigning politeness, and use the pause to hide how damned hard the stairs are for him, they're really a bitch on his bad knees. He has his tricks. Even though no one's watching anyway, he can't bear to let on that he's weak. Not even the older people notice him anymore, of course not, they're probably scared to see him so worn down. They're next, after all.

—Hey, son! I was your age once too, you know.

He can't figure out how it's come to this.

Finally the last landing. He sees the young couple.

—Oh Robby, I didn't see you there! What are you doing up here? And your friend... dangling her legs outside the window? That's crazy!

They had held hands, he remembers the laugh on the girl's face. One little push, and then there's only the square of bright empty sky framed in the open window.

The monotonous grinding noise from the workshop below suddenly stops. Everything is completely still. Are no planes flying today? Have all the cars stopped? The wind has died. No construction sounds from nearby. No children cry. Nothing moves.

—It woke everyone up, got people talking. Otherwise they'd never say a word to me, to us, to me and Bella, but for a few days after it happened, everyone wanted to say his piece. People didn't slam their doors when they saw us. And a bunch of kids sat down on the asphalt in a circle with candles where the two kids landed when they crashed down. And they did, who knows what, they did some kind of hocus-pocus...he was a nice boy though, seemed like, it was just that he had a lisp. Good morning, Herr Chlichmann...He would greet me when he saw me in the stairwell, he was the only one, even though he couldn't say the *sch* properly. He could only say Chlichmann. Good morning, Herr Chlichmann, whenever he ran into me in the building. If I had been named Lehmann, I wouldn't have even noticed the lisp, you see! He wasn't a loner at all, he had friends, I saw them sometimes, they were all perfectly normal. The mother, too. They lived together, she's a cashier in a store where I shop now and then. I found out that he'd spoken to her sometimes about suicide. But she couldn't have known, couldn't have ever imagined...it's impossible! He said that he'd rather kill himself than wait until they were all killed... By whom, son? By what?...I didn't know the girl...yes...they were a couple, you could tell! We're a couple too, Bella and I, right Bella?

The dog gets a little kick.

—She's called Bella...not because she's as loud as a bell, no...no, she's called Bella because she's so beautiful...bella Italia, I'd like to go there sometime, but it's no use anymore with my leg and my lungs, my asthma...no, but suicide, no...I can't understand it. No one can understand it. A healthy young person…! Even I'd never kill myself! Listen to me, I'm on my last gasp, and still I don't kill myself!

"Take joy in life…," he sings, and falls into a fit of coughing.

—Wait a sec, Bella.

And he starts to sing again.

"Take joy in life…as long as the candle still burns…."

There, he made it! Bella gets another kick.

—Right, Bella? We'll make it!

—See, you didn't have to do it, Robby, you didn't have to jump down with that girl and end up dead as a doornail.

—But I like it better this way, Herr Chlichmann.

—Is that what you were afraid of? That you'd never make it in life? Or what?

—I didn't want anything to do with that kind of life.

—With a life like mine, huh?…Got nothing to say to that, have you. You look away as if I were a pile of shit.

—I don't even see you, Herr Chlichmann.

—What does that mean: You don't see me. Your eyes are open!

—I don't know.

—All I want to say is that life is a gift, you don't have anything else, and it was colossal stupidity to finish it off yourself.

—I'm happier dead.

—But to be dead, that's no way to be, son, that is no way to be!

Schlichmann coughs and wheezes.

THE KING OF SPAIN. Lilly remembered it well. Her drunken mother, holding the crumpled photograph to her breast with

9

trembling hands like a holy icon: Your father, the Spaniard, the asshole, the Spanish King, she'd said, only he wasn't wearing the crown in this picture. To celebrate the occasion, she'd said, he'd decided to show off the boil on his bald head instead. Don't laugh! And then Lilly had seen her father in the flesh, on the train tracks near the broken-down cars and the unkempt vegetable garden, behind the broken railings, by the scraps of corrugated iron, where she's the leader of the gang: the gang of children with irresponsible mothers. That's where it all happened. She saw her father coming, but not on the path between the tracks. Instead, he appeared standing, bearing himself proudly upright, standing on a flatcar, riding along with his whole magnificent retinue. There he stood, and no one would have dared to say that he was only an immigrant laborer, and not the King of Spain. He stood there so regally and wore his crown and smoked cigarettes, in fact he had two burning cigarettes in his mouth at the same time, and threw them away after a few quick drags, one to the right and one to the left, and each time a flame shot up from the yellowed summer grass. He left a trail of fire in his wake. Is it true? That's how Lilly tells it. She ran after the car and stomped down the burning grass, so that the whole area didn't go up in smoke.

—What did he say to you?

—There was nothing to say, pea-brain! He was driving away from me, and since I was running I could only gasp for breath. That's how he drove to Spain, I'm supposed to come meet him later.

—I don't believe it!

The face of an old man suddenly appears outside the dirty window. He eyes the children who crouch near each other in the semidarkness and shakes his head so fast back and forth that the straps of his aviator cap flutter around his face.

—Bomber pilot! Bomber pilot! the children scream.

10

At that he disappears. His moped rattles.

—I'll shoot him! Krrrrrr! On your knees! screams the fat boy. On your knees I say, now! and he babbles on in an incomprehensible gobbledygook of childspeak, since no other good threats occur to him.

—Stop it!

Krrrrr! He mows everyone down with his plastic machine gun.

—Maxi stinks!

Lilly ignores her little brother, she rummages in the plastic bag for her tape player and her floppy ruffle skirt. She wants to do her Spanish dance.

—Turn the tape player on!

It only croaks and crackles.

—Maxi stinks!

—Whatever. Hold your nose.

Maxi starts to blubber. The tape recorder crackles.

—C'mon, play music!

Someone pushes other buttons, tries them all: rewind, fast forward, play, start, stop, and start again.

—Dance music! Dance music!

The puny redheaded girl snickers and hops on her spindly legs until one of the boys pushes her away.

Eventually the music starts. Lilly dances. She bounces stiffly and woodenly, yanks the ruffle skirt mechanically to and fro, jerks it down and then up, too suddenly. The children grow bored, stop watching, jostle each other, and begin fighting. Lilly dances solemnly on.

I CAN SEE YOU, and you don't even know it! You're walking away, now you're coming back. What's sticking out of your mouth? I can't tell, stand still for a sec. Oh, it's your toothbrush. White gunk is running down your chin. Walking around with your toothbrush sticking out, is that ladylike? And running around with a naked behind and only a dress-up jacket on top, aren't you ashamed, you think you can just get away with it, you little tart. Wind tears at the bushes outside. The angry shadows of branches slash through the scene, the bright square of the patio is only a slight shimmer behind the rain-soaked leaves. Where is she now? Come on, come on, let me see that naked ass. Yes, now, right now! Come on, bend over! Yes, bend over and pick up your shoes! You're not obeying me. You'll have to be punished. I'll think of something for you, missy! What's with the bathrobe now? Did I say you should put on your bathrobe?

Is someone there? There's no one to be seen in the front yard. Dagmar stands in the open patio door and listens into the blackness. Outside on the street the light of the curved streetlamp falls on a figure who scurries away with his coat over his head in the heavy splashing rain.

NO, IT REALLY WOULDN'T BOTHER ME if someone stood outside and peeped in at me.

—Well, it bothers me, Dagmar says crossly, yanking at the zipper of her suitcase, which has gotten stuck on a piece of clothing.

—Come on, help me, Lisa!

It wouldn't kill her to help me a little bit and not just stand there lounging around, looking at my pictures, my new photos on the glass table, trying out my precious Italian chair.

—You're more patient than I am!

She leaves Lisa to fiddle with the suitcase.

12

—He's really only peeping because of you. He'll be disappointed when he peeps in and sees that I'm staying in the apartment for a while.

—Oh, I forgot the red dress, Dagmar groans, you have to open the suitcase again.

Actually she just wants to keep Lisa from wearing her old red dress while she's away. She closes the closet door a bit too violently and for a moment considers taking the key with her. I'm funny about that sort of thing.

—You have such pretty things, she hears Lisa say rapturously.

This makes Dagmar feel bad for being so strict in her refusal, and she gives the surprised Lisa a quick kiss as she goes by.

Dagmar is my best friend. She's so nice to me! Lisa beams.

—Can't you see if you can get me a part sometime? Just a tiny little role? You know all those people in film.

—Casting isn't my thing, you know that.

Of course she knows that a film editor can't cast roles, but Dagmar, her friend, is more than just an editor, she's so pretty, surely she has influence in the production company, surely!

—Maybe they'd be more likely to take me if I didn't require a fee. You can definitely say that I don't want any money. I might not be very impressive when I'm just my normal self, like right now. But I've practiced in front of the mirror; I can look totally different.

Dagmar, busy with her departure. A quick look.

—Yeah?

The cell phone is almost dead. Where did I put the charger? The cord, the cord, umbilical cord! And the recipe, I had it in the little bag, and now where is that little bag? It's so aggravating when things aren't where they belong. The nail file…in the kitchen!

—I could act something for you, Dagmar, shall I?

—No, not now, please! You can see how busy I am, can't you?

—But when, then? We have to do it sometime.

—You're a comedian!

What does Dagmar mean by that? Lisa doesn't notice her friend's anger, she needs to be heard out no matter what.

—It doesn't have to be an important part. Surely sometime they'll need someone who just angrily runs through a room. I could do something like that! Or a comic role: someone could pour milk on my head.

—Do you think that's comic?

—First I could give a funny shriek, and then fall down.

What is she thinking, the stupid cow!

—Just don't practice the milk bit in my apartment.

—Oh no, when I'm living in your apartment, I'll be just like you, that's the best part.

—And what am I like?

A snide question. What does she know about me! Lisa gets passionate.

—Oh, I admire you so much! All the pictures and books you have! And I can invite all your friends here, I know all of them. Except Bonsack, I won't invite him.

—Oh, so you can't stand him anymore.

—Soon you'll see what he's really like.

—He really didn't suit you, Lisa.

—He was probably looking for a more intellectual woman. But still: Be careful!

—All right, I'm out.

—One can't keep him for very long anyway. A thousand affairs but no feelings.

Irritating, again. What does it matter to Lisa if I go out with Bonsack? She always compares herself to me! I need to break her of that habit. She makes one final attempt to dissuade

Lisa from moving into her apartment:

—Can you really leave your mother alone for four whole weeks?

—I'll go over every day and take care of her.

—Back and forth all the time?

—I don't mind.

Shot down! It was a mistake to offer her the apartment. I didn't actually offer. She asked, and I didn't defend myself. I'm not assertive enough. Now she's moving in.

—If I were you I'd always close the curtains all the way. Because of the Peeping Tom.

—You know, I understand him somehow, I'm actually kind of like that too. I always want to see what other people are doing.

—That's a bit different from what he's doing, Lisa!

She's already made herself a nest in Dagmar's favorite chair and is sitting with her legs up, lost in thought: I can be anything, any kind of person, I can be an old man or a really fat one, I can even be a dog or a thing! I can be a trash can, a creaky closet, I can be a birthday cake, a bird's nest, whatever I want, a thicket, a lawnmower, I can be anything I can think of.

WHO IS MALLMÖH? Lisa's mother often sits all day long in one corner of the sofa. She sits stiffly, dressed for travel, as if she's waiting for someone to pick her up and take her with him on a long journey. Sometimes she even has her hat on already, it sits flatly on her thin hair. Like a landmine, Lisa says.

—So what are you waiting for?

—I'm not waiting for anyone, Vanessa insists stubbornly.

—You never go out. You might as well be lame, the way you always sit there without budging an inch.

—I got a letter from Boston again.

—Show me.

Vanessa makes no move to show her the letter, so Lisa snaps it up from the table herself.

—I get to keep the stamp. So what does he write? Anything new?

She's too impatient to read the letter. Mother should go there sometime! He said that he'd send a ticket.

—If an old boyfriend said he'd send me a ticket, I'd fly there immediately.

—Of course you would! My daughter lacks character, Vanessa complains. Just snap your fingers and she'll do anything! A flibbertigibbet, my father would have called me, if I'd been like that. You'll go to the dogs eventually.

She lives to scold! And she has no one else, I'm really all she's got! Did she have friends before? I don't remember anyone coming to visit, I don't remember her going to the movies or for a stroll with a girlfriend. I have a lot of good friends, I can be proud of that. And when I'm as old as Mother is now... Lisa looks at herself in the mirror, puts her face very close to the glass, as if she could tell more that way, then even closer, with her tongue she can touch the cold tip of her tongue in the mirror. She looks for her old-lady face.

The two, mother and daughter, live in two furnished rooms with sloping walls accessed through a wide, empty, dimly lit attic. The entire upper floor, which once housed servants, was to have been renovated years ago, but the renovation stopped once the two half-finished adjoining rooms had been reclaimed. Lisa and her mother weren't bothered by the few exposed pipes and the uncleaned walls in the garret outside. The rooms, unprettily outfitted with the bare necessities, had been a good deal.

—I like to improvise, Lisa explains to her friends, and to

foster this impression she always leaves a pillow or a few books and magazines almost accidentally on the floor. Her mother's room looks exactly as it had when she'd moved in eight years ago: a dark table too big for the room and four chairs, their high backs shoved close to the tabletop, as if sitting is strictly forbidden. There's a sofa bed and a shabby brown leather armchair, on whose right arm a doily is laid for protection.

Vanessa had not even done so much as to construct a curtain for the room's one window. Only the black lacquered piano, placed so inconveniently in front of the sloping wall that one has to sit stooped over on the stool to play, is Vanessa's property. The only thing my mother cared about was that she could fit her piano, Lisa explains. It hasn't been tuned since we moved in, and she doesn't play it anymore, but I can still hear the plunking of her students in my ears from my childhood. And at night she played Chopin and Schubert for me, so that as I fell asleep under the cold bedcovers I'd have beautiful thoughts.

Whoever comes to visit Lisa must pass Vanessa's room, and in the warm seasons Vanessa usually keeps the door to the attic open wide enough that she can see who comes in from the sofa without having to bend over to satisfy her curiosity. Gentleman callers! she says to Lisa with raised eyebrows. What sort of creatures are they? Lisa claims that some are writers whose texts she transcribes from recordings, others she's met at parties.

—Where you just carry around the wine glasses, says Vanessa, where you're just used. A willing victim, a hanger-on.

—And you just sit on your sofa and ambush my guests, Lisa counters in rebellion. I always have to make excuses for your nosiness.

—This Herr Mallmöh, says Vanessa, I know his name, because he told me. With the funny ö, I made a note of that. He saw the door open and came in, since you weren't here. And his first sentence is: Are you Jewish? At this Vanessa had turned away from him on the sofa and said nothing more until he left. And he closed the door behind him: shameless. It's supposed to stay open!

—He couldn't have known that.

—Who is this Mallmöh?

So she's interested, she just won't admit it.

—And the one with the three-day beard is also a writer?

Writers, Vanessa asserts, can be recognized by their quiet steps.

—Albrecht was wearing Reeboks, that's why you didn't hear him on the stairs.

—I saw. Such ugly shoes.

—He's not really that quiet, he often whistles to himself. Lisa laughs, refusing to let her mood be ruined.

—He probably whistles to gather his courage, Vanessa says mockingly.

—The things you come up with, Mother! Lisa tries to explain to her that Albrecht is writing a novel and that she's helping him with it.

—You?

I tell him about experiences I've had, about strange people I've met, or he'll ask me to tell him about a luggage store, for example.

—A luggage store?

—He needs the luggage store for his novel. He's kind of inexperienced. For example, he has no idea how a woman thinks, so I have to explain it to him.

—You're no more than a typist!

Once Mallmöh came, stuck his moon-face impudently through Vanessa's door and crowed:

—Ha! Lying in ambush! She's been expecting me!

—Not me, Herr Mallmöh! My daughter, perhaps. Unfortunately I cannot hinder her.

18

—Nor understand her! Mallmöh laughs immoderately.

—You must stop frightening me with that terrible laughter of yours.

—So I'm the three hundred sixty-fifth?

—How do you get three hundred sixty-five?

—One every day. That makes three hundred sixty-five.

—Did you bring Lisa a gift?

—I just wanted to bring her back an earring.

—You tore it from her!

—No, no, Mallmöh protests, with raised hands.

—I saw her torn ear: bloody!

—No, that can't be. It's only a clip.

—What do men know of earrings!

—But I know something of women! laughs Mallmöh threateningly. His whole face, shining with oil, twists out of shape.

Here Vanessa asks slyly: Why didn't you bring me anything?

—If I had known in advance that I'd come across Lisa's mother, instead of finding her exceedingly charming daughter, I would have brought you something, my dear lady!

—Like what, for example?

—Like what...like what, murmurs Mallmöh, perplexed.

—Yes, yes, like what?

After a moment of bewilderment, Mallmöh breaks again into a giant laugh.

—Ah, says Vanessa with a charming smile, maybe a little good-luck charm?

—I'm a good-luck charm myself, my dear.

Vanessa makes no reply.

—An elephant?

—How big?

Vanessa shows him with her fragile fingers: this small, quite small!

—Gooseberry tart! trumpets Mallmöh.

—Oh yes, gooseberry tart! I can't go out, anyway.

—You can't go out?

The laughter again.

—Your laugh is very ugly.

—I'm laughing, says Mallmöh, suddenly serious and to the point, because this whole time I've been thinking that you wanted to go out, and that I was delaying you. You're in your coat and hat.

—I'm not wearing a coat.

Mallmöh seems to be in the best of moods, in fact he begins to beam.

—Don't take it so literally! One simply says that: in coat and hat! Unabashed, he bows deeply, and says to her: I'd be glad to take your hat off. May I? You only put it on because you barely have hair anymore. That explains the big secret.

Naturally, Vanessa doesn't reply.

—I can't go out in the street. Lisa has to do everything for me.

—Very nice, very nice, murmurs Mallmöh.

—What do you know! She hopes to end the conversation at that, and both are silent for a while. Mallmöh has sat himself tentatively down on the wobbly kitchen chair.

—Now I can hear her next door. She's in the room right next door!

—Lisa! Vanessa calls.

Both listen. Mallmöh stands up quickly and lays his ear against the wall as slowly and attentively as if he were trying to eavesdrop on an intimate conversation. Vanessa gets impatient. She stomps her feet on the floor a few times like an ill-bred child. He ought to listen, what she's saying is important!

—It's totally impossible, I can't go out in the street. There are all these monuments everywhere and I can't go past them, my legs just slide out from under me. I get faint in front of big monuments, I freeze! If I believed in past lives, I'd believe that I was sacrificed to the gods in an earlier life. To some huge idol. Something in me remembers, and I fall, frozen with helplessness.

—Psst! whispers Mallmöh, listening.

—Do you believe in past lives?

—Psst!

—I believe in neither a past life nor a future one.

—Uh huh, says Mallmöh impatiently.

—Lisa! Vanessa calls. She hears the door close. Again Mallmöh breaks into threatening laughter.

—Nor in the present one, either!

"FATHER, pull your son from this bloody skin and lift him to your heart."
—*Found Object*

AFTER ITS FEVERISH ATTACK, the hot summer laid itself wearily down in all the streets and squares of the city. All the people who ordinarily rush so purposefully to and fro pursuing their business and pleasure have disappeared. The stoplights change from green to red and back to green without a single car passing through the intersection. The parking spaces, marked in white on the edges of the streets, are empty. Here and there, lonely old people sit motionless on the benches of the small green spaces, sometimes under the protective tin roof of a streetcar stop. They no longer seem to be waiting for the streetcar to come. The houses with wide open windows seem forlorn, as

21

if some catastrophe had occurred, as if all had succumbed to some epidemic, or as if the threat of war had banished all the residents. Where to? To a spot where brooks gurgle and birds twitter. This beautiful place must exist somewhere, this place where the escapees gather and reunite, where they spend the time sitting on their towels and calling out to each other and reminiscing until the cool evening comes.

Vanessa lets the oil drain from the bottle and run over Lisa's shoulders. She rubs it into Lisa's hunched back with her little claws.

—Use the palm of your hand, please. You're scratching me!

—Just see what it's like when you have arthritis in your fingers!

What she'd like to say is that I'll get arthritis soon, when I'm just a few years older. She looks forward to that day.

—Isn't it beautiful here, Mother, Lisa says with emphasis.

Vanessa can hear the accusation in that, she glances quickly at the rocky riverbank, where naked people encamp on their towels, and shakes her head in disapproval:

—Over the long winter, I forgot how ugly people are!

—But I'm not ugly!

Lisa tugs her bathing suit into place. A little swivel of the hips. Knees tight together and bent to the side. Neck bent back to accentuate the breasts. A clip holds the mass of her hair. Starry eyes.

—I think I'm attractive!

Silence.

—Don't you think I'm beautiful? I'm your daughter, you have to think I'm beautiful! Clumsily, she plays to the imaginary crowd with a few coquettish movements.

—Yes. You're certainly still young.

—I have a good figure.

She notes the look of appraisal and, before Vanessa can put

in an objection, says:

—Yes, I know. A bruise. Calm down: it doesn't mean anything.

But Vanessa doesn't let it go.

—You're probably hiding welts under your bathing suit. That's why you're wearing a one-piece.

—Oh, whatever. One-pieces are stylish.

—You can't fool me.

—I'm not trying to.

—So who was the man yesterday?

Lisa already knows her complaint.

—No one can please you anyway.

— No! Vanessa sits up with a jolt. Their old quarrel.

—Just because someone likes me, you think there must be something wrong with him.

—You look like a victim. It attracts them.

That island in the river is so pretty. What a peaceful day, with the summery shrieks of children spattering about in the water and splashing each other! It's pointless to talk with Mother, I've always gone to such trouble for her, for once maybe she could just appreciate that! If she didn't have me, she'd never even get out of her garret again. Lisa balances on the hot stones on the way to the water. If only I could change her! She sits there on her towel in this beautiful place, oblivious to everything! I'll turn around now and tell her that I'm moving out for a few weeks. Only a few more steps. Ow, my feet! Hot, hot! I'll just call out to her as soon as I'm in the water. Vanessa! Vanessa! She doesn't hear me. And I don't want to know what she'll say anyway. Maybe she'll beg me to stay. No, I've never heard her beg for anything, she thinks she's too proud for that. I'm not proud. Pride is actually a really bad quality. What does she have to be proud of?

Froth, eddies. Here between the stony island and our bank

the current is really quite strong. I have to use all my strength not to be bashed about and swept away. Can't get any air! It's pushing my head under. I can't stay up! The smooth stones, I'm slipping, I can't see anything. I have to get up! I have to get up! There's the bank and the people. No one even noticed! First, just get some air. Vanessa! She's sitting, such a small, neat little person with her hat, she doesn't belong here at all. Everything is just as it was before. And I'm alive! Over there: the long line of cars, some covered with screens against the hot sun. Over there: a moped rider stands still, then rides on, bouncing over the roots of trees. It's really only a path, not a real street, he bounces as if he were on an obstacle course. Why don't you just turn off that rattling motor and walk. And now I'll just let myself fall and let the current carry me gently to the riverbank.

—Lisa!

Vanessa waves.

—Wchhhh! Says the moped man, and makes a movement like he's cracking a whip. Appalled, Vanessa turns around.

—I suppose you're a hitter?

—I was just waving and making a little sound to go along with it. Good day Madame, you can kiss my ass.

—Lisa!

Where did she get off to now? She was over by that waterfall just a moment ago.

—Lisa, Lisa! he apes with his crow voice. The moped leans against a bush. The geezer makes as if to climb down the slope and buttons his jacket over his naked belly. Vanessa sits tensely upright, her little hands balled into fists and pressed to her breast. If only Lisa were here!

—Don't think I'm alone! My daughter is just coming out of the water, and the police are here, too.

—Oh I'm just inspecting the meat, says the geezer, but I've never noticed you before, Madame, you're not in my album.

24

A hazelnut twig snaps in his face as he's climbing down. It hurts, he'll give up soon now. Was he watching her from a distance, waiting until Lisa went into the water?

—Are you an aviator?

A quick movement of the head, a quick look.

—What a compliment! I thank you for your guess.

—Because you're wearing an aviator cap.

—It's an heirloom. I have other interests. I have an album full of the most beautiful women. Shots from front and back. I'll bring it with me, when next we meet. Daliah Lavi, Marilyn Monroe, Rita Hayworth, Brigitte Bardot, famous names, all the older models. Sirikit, Soraya, Jackie, the wife of that Greek moneybags back in the day, Lollobrigida, Veronika Ferres and Verona Feldbusch, I fuck her after every episode. Julia Roberts, Claudia Schiffer and Madonna, who's no Madonna, I know what's what. Lopsy, Gabi and Ramona, them I only have from behind, and Lilly, that horny little slut, I have her in the album a couple times, but now she's thirty, not so tasty any more. You understand me, Madame?

—I'm not even listening.

Thank God Lisa is on her way back. She stumbles on the stones a few times, she can't come fast enough. From far away she calls:

—You there, get away!

The old man winks at Vanessa, unashamed, and tears the aviator cap from his head, gives a sort of bow.

—Farewell, you rusty old screw. Your humble Fritz with the aviator cap bids you adieu.

HELLO LISA! The jostling crowd causes the full glasses on the tray to rattle.

Careful! Oh Albrecht, it's you! I should have known you'd be the one to knock me off balance.

She beams at him. But the young man, his chest bare under a linen jacket, is unmoved. He's not that young anymore, really.

—Listen, you!

He's already drained the glass and given it quickly back to her.

—At least it's better than this stuff on the walls!

This gets a rise out of Lisa.

—Hey, he just had incredible success in New York!

—Don't just repeat the bullshit you hear around here! He gets very close to her face. With his teeth, he carefully pulls out a strand of hair that curls out of Lisa's updo. Just because you get to carry the glasses around and are always trying to be a part of things, he says crossly.

—You're here too!

—Unfortunately! It was a mistake!

But of course he's not leaving, he wants to be here too! In any case, no one is looking at the pictures on the wall anymore. At first there had been the feigned surprise, the opportune and thoughtful "Aha's" and the glances of connoisseurs from picture to picture. Then people had given themselves over to the usual small talk. Hugs, nods, shrill laughter.

—"Les Chimères du Monde," or something like that.

—Tell me, Hans, isn't that the name of the fabulous restaurant on the Île? "Les Chimères du Monde"?

—Write that down, Anna! A trouvaille, says Bonsack to his wife. "Les Chimères du Monde"!

Lisa is annoyed that Anna looks at him so admiringly, her head titled to the side.

—Are you happy, Lisa?

Albrecht and his stupid questions! How can one ask such a question, and with such a look on his face! As if he needed her answer for research purposes, as if something depended on her answer! No wonder everyone finds him exhausting. He's just awkward and thinks his nosiness makes him interesting. I know it! She really should explain to him sometime that people are just annoyed by his interrogations, and therefore do whatever they can to get out of his way when he comes at them with his intense face.

—Are you happy here?

Of course she's happy to be here, happy to hear all the voices, the tangle of voices, loud voices that she knows, she's happy to be around people who can maneuver so sleekly in the world.

—I'm deep, deep in your debt!

—Certainly not!

—New York, L.A., Basel, of course, Paris hardly…London will come again…

—No, no. I'm not a romantic! Adamant, dismissive hands. Hearty laughter.

—Yes, a lot…far too much traveling…for business as well.

—Weekends, five days at most.

—I'm paid too much for that.

- Later? What does that mean. There won't be a later.

And the lady who's turned around and sailed over to Mallmöh with "Youyouyou. I've found you, you naughty thing, you!" And kisses him on both ears, as he tries to save his glass. "You're being shaken and stirred, youyouyou!"

It's incredible that Dr. Mallmöh, a hotshot lawyer, would put up with this kind of attack! Would he put up with that from me? They're all such original people here, no poseurs! It's funny, how desperately he's balancing the glass in his outstretched hand, high above his head. I'll go fetch it, otherwise he'll slop the wine all over his jacket.

—Hello Lisa!

Things certainly can't be this lax in his office, his secretary must make sure of that. This place has a special vibe. She has to stretch—on tiptoes she's just able to snatch the glass. She wants to say something witty, but nothing occurs to her at the moment. So she simply beams at him ardently, her dark-red painted mouth open, baring the teeth she's so proud of since the time Fred told her she had the mouth of a predator...such a pretty predator's mouth! It's just too bad you don't bite. What did he mean by that? I'm just not the aggressive kind, I'm sorry.

—Lisa! Lisa!

She hurries, she still has to pass around the canapés.

—How is that pronounced: Aleijadinho?

—Just how it's written.

—Ale-jadin-ho, Anna tries carefully.

—Aleijadinho, Bonsack corrects her in melodic Brazilian, his accent meticulous.

—A little cripple, he was, Anna hurries to add. Adam has written wonderfully about this artist. About his tragic life.

—Not about his life. I've tried to write something about his art.

Albrecht inserts himself into the conversation.

—Can one separate the two, then?

—It's a really thrilling text, Anna says quietly, her head lowered. In her gentle tone there's a clear rebuke of his meddling.

But he doesn't give up.

—I'll have to decide for myself whether the text is thrilling. Bonsack smiles arrogantly, defending himself with feigned humility.

—It's just a little essay, nothing for the public at large. Anna's exaggerating again. And since Anna loyally keeps quiet, he adds: Out of love. It sounds scornful.

28

ALEIJADINHO. In his thirtieth year, when he had already begun his greatest work, he discovered that he was afflicted with leprosy. He saw the white spots on his skin. He continued to work unfalteringly on the great stone sculpture until his fingers grew numb. The flesh began to disintegrate, holes and caverns formed. When both hands rotted off, he had his tools strapped to the stumps of his arms, the chisel on the left, the hammer on the right. In this way he could keep working. When his legs could no longer carry him, when finally legs and feet had rotted away, he bought a black slave, on whose shoulders he perched and continued to work. By this time he had formed a Mt. Calvary full of figures. He was now the most famous artist in Brazil. More and more people who admired his art came and wanted to watch how he carved beautiful figures out of stone blocks: saints and criminals, sufferers, soldiers, angels and animals. Because of his disfiguration people now called Aleijadinho: "the little cripple." As his face was more and more devastated by the leprosy, as nose, lips, and ears rotted away, the onlookers were repulsed, because it reminded them of their mortality, and his sponsor wanted him to give up the work. But Aleijadinho had a leather sack made with two holes for his eyes, and he put this over his face. Finally the work was done, the Mt. Calvary completed. Its creator was nothing more than a pile of filth and stench. The pious and the admirers pushed the nauseating bundle on the steps aside. But his head cried out the glory of God, because God had let him complete his work.

THE NERVOUS MAN pushes a pair of glasses up on his head, breathes on, licks, and dries a second pair with a scrap of paper, puts them on, then fingers his breast pocket for a third pair.

—I see catastrophic disorder on my desk; it's overloaded with bescribbled papers, photos, notes, unanswered letters, hotel bills, magazine clippings, telephone numbers and addresses on scraps of paper. The Georgian student that cleans for me tries every week, in her fastidious love of order, to do away with this chaos, but I say to her: Change nothing! In fact, the thought has come to me that this seemingly arbitrary juxtaposition and layering, the whole chaos on my desk, corresponds to the chaos of the Creation, it has come to pass similarly, yes indeed, willed to be thus by the universal spirit. It is with this thought that I've begun to believe in miracles. Miracles, he says, as he rubs his glasses again, are indeed the outcome of disorder. The orderly can't abide miracles; to the disorderly they are the triumph of the imagination over reason. Why can't a ladder, as Jacob dreamed, reach to heaven?

AND? Her fearful, pinched look. The boy doesn't look at her, he stands there next to the little marble table, looks at the empty coffee cup, simply shrugs his shoulders. She shoves the coffee cup fiercely aside. There's nothing to see there, look your mother in the eye! She'd already waited so long in the dreary little café for his return, had observed the house across the street through the snarled leaves of potted plants, until finally he came out and slowly, so slowly, sauntered across the square. As if none of this even concerned him! Come back already, hurry now, Bertie! I'm waiting, I want to know what you've found out!

—And? Did you go up to the apartment door?
He nods.
—Did you ring three times?
He nods.
—But he didn't open the door!
He nods.

—Did you listen at the door? Was anything moving in the apartment? At least look at me and stop staring idiotically at the table!

As the waiter takes the empty coffee cup away, she throws him a beseeching look: What's to be done with a son who refuses to even answer?

—Do you have children?

The waiter flutters the crumbs off the table.

—I didn't want the burden.

—I can talk with you, at least! she says. We've sat for three hours now in this café, and who knows if we'll even catch a glimpse of his face!

—He was here yesterday.

—How does he look now?

—He looks quite normal, says the waiter, shrugging his shoulders.

—What do you mean, normal?

—You know, normal. Normal is normal.

—Normal, you say? That's shameless, she thinks, he really thinks I'm the crazy one! But she won't give up.

—When he sits here in the café, is he somehow…I mean, peculiar?

He doesn't want to get into this.

—No, quite normal.

Stay calm, keep quiet! Just don't get too aggressive! Finally the question:

—He comes alone?

—Always alone.

—Does he speak to you?

—He speaks little.

Clear the air, she thinks, eat something, order something else.

—Would you like another ice cream, Bertie? The boy nods.

—Bring the boy another ice cream.

As the waiter comes back with the ice cream, he says: The man spoke once of electricity. That must be his field.

—Oh, come now. He's a lawyer! He's a legal advisor in an investment firm! Yes, he is! In Hannover! We live in Hannover, actually. And here he is, claiming to be something else entirely. That shows how odd he is. That's really odd, you must admit! She talks and talks. She talks much too much, her nervousness pulses through the room. What does the waiter care if we live in Hannover! Why am I describing our house to him? Semidetached, sauna, and the problems with the hot water heater? A heater these days only lasts fifteen years, can you imagine? I have to stop talking! But instead, she talks faster and faster. Bertie spoons up his pink ice cream. Don't eat so mechanically! She's so irritable she'd like to slap his hands. You spoon it up like a machine! He rented an apartment in the building over there, half a year ago, I didn't know that at first. I know absolutely nothing. Imagine! No discussion, no letter, no news, absolutely nothing. What do you think?

What a question! The waiter stands there with crossed arms, shrugs his shoulders apologetically, and listens. Now, near evening, there are no other patrons in the Blue Diamond anyway. In less than half an hour he can close. The tables are all wiped off and the ice cream menus, the tea menus, the lunch special for tomorrow (Königsberg meatballs, side of quark $4.95) are all straightened in their wire holders. The remaining cakes and pastries have been assembled on a tray. Tomorrow they'll be sold for half price.

—Everyone asks me, and I know nothing. What should I tell them? His mother asks me, and what can I tell her? And his brother, and the people from his office? They all ask me! At first I thought they'd let him go. But they hadn't. He just stopped going. Then I made something up, an accident. He was on family business. In Mexico. He went on the spur of the

32

moment. I just made it up. What do you think of that?

—I was in Mexico once too, says the waiter. Death is very important in their culture. There are even death's heads made of icing.

—Back then I still thought, after a while he'll resurface. Then it occurred to me that a little while ago he'd said to me: I have to go. I have to go a different way. I didn't think he was serious. How could I? Even that makes him sound crazy. What do you think? The job...he had such a good job, in such a good company...these days...and the house and everything... and him! What is our Bertie to do! I had thought before that maybe he should get therapy. Or could it be another woman?

—There he goes!

—He's wearing the blue coat! What a dumb observation! Go over! Quick! Go over to him, Bertie! She takes the ice cream away from the boy. Pink drops fall from the spoon that the boy holds in the air.

—In a sec. I'll just wait a bit.

—It's dripping! Look! She tears the spoon nervously from his hand. You act like a four year old, and you're almost sixteen!

AND FROM ME YOU WANT...WHAT?

The boy slumps uncomfortably on the only chair in the room, gripping the seat with both hands. He tries to dodge his father's stern eyes, but his gaze finds nowhere to rest, the apartment is white and empty. The window before him is hung with white sheets.

—My mother wants me...me...and her....

—Yes, what, what?

—Stationery store, the boy murmurs, and when his father doesn't react, he adds: with lotto.

—She wants to open a stationery store, or buy one, or what?

—There's one for sale and they're looking for someone to run it.

—So.

—Thirty thousand to settle.

—She wants that from me?

—Then she won't need any more money.

—Paper…fill paper up with words and throw it away… paper….

—There's a school close by. It'll do well. They say it's a sure thing.

—School…where old lies get rechewed and spit out and you gobble them up…. Why do you go to school, son?

—I'm already out of school. I just finished.

The father goes wordlessly into another room, comes back and stands directly in front of the boy. He examines him with raised eyebrows from over the frame of his glasses, then moves slowly backward without shifting his gaze.

—You only have one chair, says Bertie.

—Yes, and my son is sitting in it! says Bissmeier. With expensive braces in his mouth. Straightening his teeth!

Bertie slides irresolutely to the edge of the chair.

—Sit! Sit! I'm always moving. The thinking man doesn't slump in a chair and brood. He moves here and there, back and forth, as you see. Do you see?

—Yes.

—I don't need a second chair. I have no visitors. There's no one to blabber, no one to fill the room with nonsense.

As if to free himself from a choking cloud of dust, he blows into the air with puffed cheeks. Ffffff.

This is funny, Bertie wants to laugh, but careful, careful!

—What I need, says Bissmeier sternly, is emptiness and silence. Purity, if you can grasp that. There's nothing pure left

34

in the world. Everything has been dirtied, the water is dirty even at the source, the stones are dirtied, the souls...dirty! Only the assassin lives in purity. There's a paradox for you!

—No.

—Do I have a sword? A Damascus blade so sharp that it could split a white sheet of paper as easily and unhesitant as if it were mere water? Or is there a bomb here? Nothing of the sort. Perhaps just some scissors. Or a pencil, sharp as an arrow. Or my fingernail, look at it: dangerously sharp! I've chosen it from the ensemble of my fingers. Not my thumb! Don't pretend, don't worry, I can see from your eyes that you don't understand me. You understand nothing at all! How could you know anything! The world is full of false information. And your mother, is she waiting downstairs?

With a surprising leap Bissmeier springs to the window. He pushes the white cloth carefully aside.

—She's standing there in the square!

—Yes, says Bertie unnecessarily, thereby angering his father.

—You're accomplices, you're trying to trap me.

—No, says Bertie.

—I confess, yells Bissmeier in a mournful voice, and tugs so fiercely at his jacket that a button springs off. I confess that I have neglected to open my son's eyes to the truth. But the end is now coming into view. What end, you ask.

—I didn't ask anything.

Bertie bends down to pick up the button, but before he gets it, his father covers it swiftly with his foot.

—The absolute end. The absolute, final end.

Why does he yell like that?

He'd begun the speech grandly, but now he breaks off in the middle and all at once it's dead quiet. Somewhere water gurgles in a pipe.

Bertie uses the long silence to make one more attempt: thirty thousand.

—So, you're going to be a businessman!

—Yeah, well.

—You two are planning for the future. You think you're up for it? Well! The "well" is thrust out like a threat, so that Bertie gets shy again and says softly: I can pitch in a little. Help out here and there.

Lights out, darkness. Through the sheets on the window, a red gleam presses in from outside. Is something burning? The father is no longer there, where has he disappeared to so quickly?... Father! No answer, no footsteps, no breathing. The silence hums in Bertie's head. I have to get the thirty thousand, I can't leave. In the hollow of his hand he carefully lights a cigarette.

—Do you see me?

The voice comes from another room. What a stupid game. Why is he playing this stupid game with me?

—No. Or maybe I should say yes. Whatever.

Suddenly it's bright, bright. A white brightness in his eyes. What's happened? His father starts screaming bloody murder, crawls on the floor near the chair, shouts, tries to push a tiny line of cigarette ash onto a tissue but it's too weak, so the ash falls and makes a gray spot on the carpet. The doorbell rings. Why is he so excited, there are other spots on the carpet already.

—You could have held your hand under it!

—I did!

—Did not!

—It was just three drags.

The doorbell rings. He crushes the cigarette out in the foil of the wrapper.

—Put your hand out!

—What for?

He puts his palm out anyway. His father hits it with unexpected fierceness. Thirty thousand! The doorbell rings. Thirty thousand in your outstretched hand! But by now the boy has already stuck his hands back under his armpits.

—Piece of shit! the father rails. The doorbell rings. Bertie leaps up and opens the door. It's his mother. His father waves his hands defensively in front of his face and screams: The doorbell is broken!

—Bertie opened the door for me.

They immediately begin to fight, and don't even notice that Bertie has slipped away.

"FEELINGS must be eradicated. Love makes one helpless. All desire for beauty and pleasure must disappear. My name must disappear. No one can know who I am. I must make myself insensitive to pain, I must bear my pain as if it were another's pain, a pain that has nothing to do with me. I must sleep without dreaming. I must not dress conspicuously. I must have no friends, and no one to help me. I must have no family, no son. No Bertie! And I must own nothing expensive, or even look at anything expensive. No! I must own nothing at all! I must remain a stranger. Be a stranger to yourself! Have no personal opinion. Confirm the opinions of others, even if they are repugnant to you. I must erase my memories. I can allow myself no judgments, save one. I may not defend myself from accusations. If someone says to me: You are an assassin! I just smile. I must not leave behind anything in my own handwriting except for this note, which contains the most important rules of conduct. I must not remember that I was ever a child. I must not even think about my age. In front of me and behind me everything shall be erased!"

These words were written in severe, businesslike handwriting on the piece of cardboard that he had taken out of a freshly pressed and folded shirt. Because he thought that this might be the sum of his insights and could perhaps later be a kind of legacy for future generations, as well as a certain explanation for his actions, which would doubtless be puzzling to many, he had placed his signature underneath, as on a document: "Bissmeier." And in front of his name a hastily scribbled "signed."

ARE YOU LISTENING, VANESSA?

—I'm listening to you, but I'm not interested in whatever your lover is saying.

—Ha, lover! laughs Mallmöh, sounding like the devil.

The threesome sits on the uncomfortable chairs at the table. Lisa had quickly removed the ugly plastic lace tablecloth and put out a plate of cookies. That's all Vanessa's thrifty conscience will allow: Lisa shouldn't always be acting as if we're millionaires. Mallmöh doesn't fail to notice the tension, he enjoys embarrassing situations, especially when he's the cause of them. Now he wants to continue his story.

—Please listen, Mother!

—True story. I render only the facts, Mallmöh assured them. When was this? The sixties? Probably. Earlier or later, doesn't matter. Right, ladies? This story came to me from an old man, an actor. Actors are never to be believed, but they always want to preach truth, those professional liars! The water glass shakes in his hands. Might I have another cookie...?

Lisa is listening so intently, she hasn't even noticed that the plate is empty. Even her mother has taken her hands from her ears. She starts to stand up.

—I've got it, Vanessa!

The rest of the time she lets Lisa serve her, she won't lift a finger. Why does she suddenly want to play the hostess? An interesting little triangle we have sitting here, thinks Mallmöh.

—I believe that you judge all of your experiences in terms of whether they would make useful stories, Herr Mallmöh.

Lisa dumps the remaining cookies onto the plate.

—Delicious, my lovely, says Mallmöh with a wink, and munches the dry biscuit.

—You could have spared the "lovely," Vanessa says poisonously. She's annoyed that her daughter is so well received by this disagreeable man. What does she have to offer? Her pretty teeth. That's all that a man could like about her. There's nothing dainty or delicate about her, none of the qualities that made men like me. By now Mallmöh is in the middle of his story, Vanessa didn't catch the beginning, she was too busy thinking about herself. How they adored me, how I was worshipped! A man in front of me on his knees, his arms full of tea roses, so many he can't even hold them all, a few have fallen on the floor. Lisa! Lisa is making goo-goo eyes at this Mallmöh, with her mouth agape she listens to him, full of such maudlin passion that she looks like an idiot. What's he saying, anyway?

—...and since it was a Pole she was lying in bed with, a *Fremdarbeiter*, as one said then, her husband could get his revenge. "I've come from the front," he says...he was a lieutenant in the SS. She was picked up immediately and the children were sent to a home. He got a divorce, just as a formality. Three years after the end of the war my friend gets a call from her. How's it going? He's back, she says. Who? Heinz. What, that swine, the SS criminal who sent you to the camp? Yes, she says, he just got out of prison in Russia. Yes. And? After a pause: I'm marrying him again...He thought he must have misheard. That can't be. He's a cripple, do you understand? she whispers into the phone, one leg is amputated, and his lungs are kaput. He screamed into the phone: I don't want to hear your sob story, stop! Just stop! Silence. Then: he's going to die soon, do you understand? A few more months, a year at most. And then I'll get the pension, I have to get at least that much from him. And she actually married him again! One year, two years, three years, she arranges her whole life around his impending death. Nothing is forgiven. He knows that she's waiting. But he doesn't die. *She* dies! What a riot! screams Mallmöh and breaks into his immoderate laughter.

—I don't know what you mean by that at all, Lisa says faintly. I find that story just awful.

Mallmöh kisses her hand and says with a grin that, to Vanessa, looks like an ambush:

—You're pretty, my little Thumbelina.

HAPPINESS. I demand my right to unhappiness! shouts Bonsack. I'm in search of an abyss to hurl myself into.

ATTEMPT NUMBER ONE AT ALEIJADINHO. Setting out from Ouro Preto early in the morning amid thick white fog: The viceroy with noble and ignoble companions, holy men in robes who must be kept cool with fans, barefoot monks, the pallid, decadent Portuguese, hollowed by tropical fevers, ladies, matrons, and whores, burros, slaves, and fleas. And everything they haul along: sausages, bread, fruit, wine, lentil porridge, roasted chickens, coconuts, tablecloths, fine silverware and parasols. Aleijadinho runs ahead, flinging his arms around to wave away the already dissipating plumes of mist, again and again he turns impatiently around, runs on, higher and higher. It will be here! They stand on the mountain, it's high noon. The surrounding earth falls away in great waves, as if the earth itself is breathing deeply in and out. The colorful company is alone at the peak of the mountains. Nothing has been created here yet, man has not yet left a trail of blood. The song of life's pain and joys is still unsung. Aleijadinho, however, can see before him what will arise here: It will be a place of pilgrimage, and the long steps up to the church will be edged with scenes of the Passion of the son of God. The path has two hundred steps, toilsome to climb, toilsome to carry the cross. Lord, pull your son from this bloody skin and lift him to your heart. You'll have to live a hundred years, the viceroy says to Aleijadinho, to conjure from this stone all the figures that you have in your head. Fifty will do, answers Aleijadinho. *Bastan cinquenta*. The whole text is in Brazilian, his mother was a black slave. The vernacular.

Isto só consegue quando Deus não põe seu pé no meu corpo, se não me morre nemhum filho, ou melhor ainda, se não me nace nemhum, se eu não me enamoro demais vezes, ou melhor: nunca! Se o meu braço não se arranca, ou pelo menos somente o esquerdo! Fome nem é tão ruim, guerra e política vocês podem manipular como quizerem. Mas quando um artista ruim, como tu és (dito para um admirador) me amola demasiado tempo com adulações, então vou necessitar duzentos anos!

Which means: Fifty will do! All I need is luck. It will only succeed if God does not stand in my way, if none of my children die, or, better yet, if I don't even have children, if I don't fall in love too often, or better yet, not at all! If my arm doesn't break off, or at least just the left one! Starvation isn't so bad. You can fight wars and run politics as you like. (And to a man who stares in awe:) But if a lousy artist like you delays me with flattery, I'll need two hundred years!

FRITZ STANDS THERE. Got anything to eat?

Lilly darts the man a quick, hostile look. He stands in the

41

door of the darkened bedroom, looking disheveled in a baggy undershirt and holey socks, twirling the straps of his old leather aviator cap. She doesn't answer.

—What are you stirring in that pot?

Then the hoarse voice from the darkness behind him:

—Lilly! What's going on?

Rattling and buzzing and wailing.

—This pudding is for Maxi!

—*I* should have it, I'm the father!

The geezer snatches the pot away from Lilly and begins to shovel the pudding down his throat with the wooden cooking spoon. Shots are fired. The crash of a violent collision, the screech of a skidding car. Who's screaming? One policeman ducks into hiding, two others jump from the patrol car, leaving the doors open. More shots.

—Then there will be nothing for Maxi! Maxi will only get cookies.

—Fine then, cookies! yells the old man over the din. Give him cookies. There are still plenty of cookies in the cupboard! And he continues to shovel the pudding into his toothless mouth. The mother in the dark room whimpers: The dirty bastard...dirty bastard.... Something falls to the floor, shatters. There's more indistinct babbling.

Now the old man has discovered the grocery bag, packed full, and asks threateningly:

—What all have you crammed in there?

—It's all mine.

—Show me!

He doesn't wait for an answer, he snatches the bag from her hands and rummages through it, pulling out everything he finds.

—Sleeping pills...oatmeal...jam...knife. Is that yours, the knife?

—Yes, it's mine. Give it here!

—I'll keep this.

—Give it here, screams Lilly, enraged. I bought that with my money.

—Your money! Your money! You don't have any money!

—I have money!

—Oh, you have money? Money you earned with your little chicken-ass!

More shots and breaking glass while they bicker over the plastic bag.

—I'm taking it with me. I'm going away.

In the darkened room something moves, a chair falls over, there's a whistling sound.

—Fritz keeps touching me! He's touching me again!

Will the mother come out of her cave now?

The man with the aviator cap tries to placate her with a grin.

—Don't be alarmed in there, my sweet. Your Lilly is just being a little princess again. All I did was lick the pot. Vanilla.

He sits there polishing off the pudding, not minding that Lilly stands before him, her face contorted with fury, watching his every move.

—I'm glad you're not my father! Just Maxi's.

—Quiet, you rat!

—If I had a father like you, I'd—I'd never stand for it!

—Shut up, you don't have any father at all.

An alarm wails. On TV, a cartoon man whines in a phony voice full of comic despair: Ah, how early I have to wake up to get all my business done. That's not necessary, says the nice young clerk from Commerzbank: We'll take care of everything for you!

—Ha! Right! The King of Spain! I know all about it! the old man jeers. He's eaten the pot clean, he flings the wooden spoon so fiercely over the table that it falls off the edge and clatters to the floor.

—Pick it up! He catches Lilly by her thin little neck and bends her over. Pick it up, Princess!

Lilly squirms away and pummels the jeering man with her little fists, bursting with anger.

—The name you can trust on every corner! The deep sound of a heavy motor covers the sonorous voice.

—Just wait, you rat. I'll catch you yet!

He manages to catch her thin, bare arm and bends it backward, contorting her face with pain.

LILLY'S LONG JOURNEY to her father in Spain. She's stolen three hundred euros out of the kitchen cupboard, where her mother keeps her money in a green metal box, hidden from the man with the aviator cap. Lilly has portioned the money meticulously: For every day she's allotted twenty marks, so that the money will last till Spain, until she gets to the king's palace, the Escorial. That's where her father lives, she's found out. She has to be sure to find the right one: She's heard from someone who's been there before that he rarely appears in person. He sends doppelgängers who look almost exactly like him. They wear a crown and sit there, nodding at visitors. She won't let herself be fooled, though. Her father will see to it that she has more money than she can possibly spend. People she meets on the road sometimes slip her something, even though she always says that she doesn't need any money. But now and then you'll have to buy something for the little one, diapers, milk, strained carrots. I don't need any money, Lilly says, and adds quickly: This way no one can take anything from me.

—Who's taking something from you, sweetheart?

She answers:

—Foreigners!

Now and then she earns a few euros, sometimes by doing some little service (Maxi always has to be there though, she can't leave him alone). Sometimes too she secretly pinches Maxi so that he screams, and she holds him in her arms and puts on her most pathetic face (an expression that's very close to her normal one, but ends up seeming more angry than distressed). And once, a woman in a wheelchair waved her over, and, without asking for any service or favor, pressed fifty euros into her hand with the words: Take this, child, I'm so happy today! She must have been crazy.

She stands on the Autobahn. The cars shoot by, racing to their distant goals like bullets, aimed to destroy. Here no one can drive slowly or stop to pick up the two poor children on the roadside. Whereto, anyway? Maybe their chances would be better in the parking lot near the highway. There are two tractor trailers and one Toyota over at the far side near the dumpsters and the restrooms. Maxi needs new Pampers. The Toyota's headlights are off. Let's just see if someone's in there. Lilly walks around the car. The driver sits stiffly behind the wheel, motionless as a doll. Lilly knocks on the window. The driver doesn't move. But she doesn't give up, she knocks and presses her face against the window. Is he dead? No, now he turns his head and looks wide-eyed at Lilly. But he doesn't roll down the window. So Lilly tries something different: The back door opens. Quickly, without saying a word, she maneuvers Maxi onto the backseat and pushes herself in after. The driver is taken by surprise. He swats at Lilly with a newspaper that had been lying next to him, as if she were an annoying fly, all without saying a word. Lilly crouches down into the cushions and finally the man stops hitting her.

—You can screw me, Lilly says.

And as the man continues to stare at her without answering, she says grimly and matter-of-factly, as if it were a threat:

—And if you don't want to, I'll take pictures.

—Take pictures why?

Lilly is already rummaging in her plastic bag and pulls out a Polaroid camera. The man hits it angrily out of her hand.

—I don't want to be photographed! Get out! Beat it!

—The door is jammed, says Lilly, and doesn't stir from her spot.

—No it isn't! You locked it! Pull the knob back up!

—I can't.

—Cheap tricks, screams the man, I hate this! I hate the brainless, disgusting tenacity with which people try to get a little advantage.

—Do you have children? Lilly asks calmly.

The question confuses him. Does he have to answer the brat? He presses his lips together so tightly that they begin to tremble.

—Do you have children? Lilly asks again.

—A son! he bursts out angrily.

—How old is he?

—Aren't you the little detective. You want to interrogate me! Secret! Secret! I truly don't know how old my son is. Should I admit that? There's not a son in the world as stupid as Bertie. He wants to sell paper! Paper, white paper and notebooks that get befouled with the writing of students, and magazines. Magazines with red headlines. What does it say? Shaking with agitation he tears the newspaper to pieces. Total darkness. The light is gone. Suddenly, his finger jabs out, pointing. Who's that there? he asks in astonishment, as if he hadn't yet noticed Maxi.

—Maxi's sleeping.

—You're like lice, like vermin! You want to bore into my skull and eat my thoughts!

Now he sits there, exhausted.

—Do you see those power lines over there? The telephone pole?

—I see them.

—I'll cut through them! I'll chop them! Then there'll be complete darkness here. The city must fall into darkness. An irrevocable last warning!

—Total darkness? Lilly asks, interested. For how long?

This alarms the man: Be quiet! Be quiet! Shut your mouth!

—But it's *you* who's been talking this whole time, not me.

—What have I said?

Lilly is careful.

—I don't know. I didn't understand anything.

—If you say anything to anyone, says the man in a flutter of agitation, I'll kill you.

—I think you're a murderer, I can see it in you. Give me a twenty.

—You little shit!

—Hush money, says Lilly in a calm voice. You can trust me. And if you have any sleeping pills, I'll take them too. For Maxi, for traveling.

The man makes no reply. A huge tractor trailer passes the window and swings onto the highway.

—So where do you want to go?

—To Spain.

This makes the man laugh.

—You want to sunbathe? Have you booked a beachfront hotel?

—I don't need a hotel. I'm going to see my father.

—Aha.

—My father is the king there.

—Baloney! Baloney!

—Whatever. All that matters is that you start driving already.

Now the man discovers the large spot on the upholstery. Maxi peed.

—Get out, you pigs! Pigs, both of you!

Like lightning he springs from the car, tears the back door open, pulls Lilly and Maxi angrily out and throws the plastic bag and the camera after them: Pigs!

Maxi begins to blubber. Lilly calmly gathers her things.

—Dumbass!

She'll say nothing about her real father to the next person who picks her up.

AROUND THE WORLD! Through countries and continents, dearie. That's why we bought the RV. And you?

—To Madrid.

—How lovely! she exclaims enthusiastically.

—We've all got wanderlust! The well endowed Rheinlander is sitting on her camping chair and feeling quite cheerful. She'd just been reading *Us* and saw lots of photos of happy people in southern resorts and magnificent ballrooms. This makes her happy too. Moved, she looks at the little traveler and her small brother. What a touching pair they are. Out of curiosity she's taking a little ramble, exploring the campsite, an hour free from parents. She just appeared suddenly by the bushes. Does she want to eat with them, no thank you, she doesn't. Her parents won't allow that. She sits very modestly on the camping chair, a very polite little lady.

—I've read about lucky coincidences, what was her name, she was called...princess of...of...and she looks at her husband beseechingly, but he just raises his hand gently in defense: Pah.

—Surely you've read about it too, child? It's in *Us*.

—I'm not allowed to read tabloids, says Lilly with lowered eyes.

—What?

—My parents don't allow it.

—That's *very* sensible! exclaims the well-endowed woman, and the man raises his hand again limply: Pah. But she doesn't give up:

—She had such a terrible childhood but then everything turned out perfectly. That's exactly what happened! Clear as the nose on your face. She was swapped as a baby and then finally someone discovered who she really was! Just by coincidence, too. And then everything was a dream. Toys, pretty dresses, pretty jewelry, a huge birthday party, a good school and lots of friends....

—I like to go to school too, says Lilly, her little lips grimly pinched.

—There, you see! And then along comes a handsome, rich and very clever young man, and it's true love! They live happily ever after.

—Pah, says the man, who's been listening, spellbound.

—I showed it to you, I even read you a bit, says the woman reproachfully. It was in *Us*.

At this the man lowers his head as if caught. He'd forgotten.

—And she had children too, of course. They were beautiful children, gifted and happy. And even when she got old she was still beautiful and healthy, she even went swimming.

—Oh swimming, the man counters cautiously, you don't know that.

—No, I read it!

—Well I certainly don't want to go swimming! asserts the man, as if thereby proving his point. This annoys the woman.

—I'd love to swim, if I still could.

—Where? Where? jeers the man.

—In the surf. In the waves.

And Lilly looks at the woman and the man and says:

—I've never been to the ocean.

—Yes, dear child, says the woman, softening, I hope that someday there's a story that nice about you in *Us*.

—Fairy tales, mutters the man, you shouldn't believe everything you hear.

—Daddy says things like that sometimes, you have to forgive him.

Daddy, daddy. Soon she'll be asking: So who is *your* daddy? What a mess! Lilly keeps the king of Spain to herself. She likes the camper. She'd like to travel in a camper, too.

—My parents wanted to buy one too, but then suddenly all their money was gone. Stolen!

—Well I never! cries the old man, and hits the camping table so fiercely that the glasses bounce.

—Let me tell you why we're traveling with the camper, explains the Rheinlander with ceremonial gravity. It's because of daddy. You see, Daddy's losing his memory. Imagine. Not between today and tomorrow, but faster and faster, the doctor said. Right, Daddy?

—Right you are.

—And so we decided to travel together. We're going on another Grand Tour. We want to see everything there is to see. From Turkey, where we've already been, up north to Norway.

—Pamukkale! cries the man, happy that the word came to him.

—And we take pictures of everything, and Daddy's always in them, so that later I can show him: You were there! We already have over 100 photos.

—Pamukkale!

—And we'll take a picture of you too, little lady, as a memento.

50

—No, Lilly counters, not of me!

—She's such a plucky little girl, isn't she, Daddy?

The man had been bending over Maxi and now quickly stood up.

—The dwarf is sleeping very deeply, he announces. He's probably dead.

—He says such awful things, but you mustn't take him seriously! And while the two elders bend over Maxi, Lilly snatches the set of camping utensils from the table. Did the man see? He turned around suddenly. He probably saw, but he says nothing. He looks at Lilly with a roguish smile.

—The place is called Pamukkale, remember that.

At that, Lilly lifts Maxi up from the ground and excuses herself politely: I think I have to go now, otherwise my parents will leave without me.

—I wouldn't worry about that!

SOMETIMES SOMEONE ASKS HER: How old are you? Then she makes herself two, three years older, so that she's not picked up and they're both sent home. Since she discovered that people allow themselves to be lied to so easily, she's invented stories about herself and Maxi, she's invented a family so kind-hearted and understanding that her listeners are moved and happy to hear it. Just as long as it's nothing bad! Nothing about the broken house near the switch yard, nothing about the shouting and the beer bottles all over the floor, nothing about the green box from which she'd taken money, nothing about the mother with the scraggly hair, nothing about the dark room. If she told about the bad things, people would become suspicious, she thinks, and tell the police. Only once was it really dangerous for her: when she told the nice old bald man who picked her up the truth about her father.

—The king of Spain? So he must have a crown on his worthy old head? He had taken his hands from the wheel and touched his own bald head, as if putting on a crown.

—He probably puts it on every morning at breakfast.

—I think so.

—And what about in the bathtub?

Is he serious? She has to laugh about the king in the bathtub.

—I imagine, muses the bald man, that such a king has a stressful life. What do you think he does from morning to night?

—He has lots of servants.

—So you think he has time to think of his little princess?

—He wrote and invited me.

—How nice! Can you show me the letter?

—I wouldn't show it to anyone!

—You're right, my little princess! He lays his arm around her in a friendly way and swerves the car back and forth, so that Lilly nearly falls against his shoulder. I wouldn't show a letter like that to anyone else either.

What luck! If I had been forced to show him the letter, what would I have said? It was stolen? Lost somewhere? She thinks quickly through all the possible lies. The more she thinks, the surer she is that she's really kept the letter and hidden it in some unknown place. Bald-Head seems satisfied with her explanation, or in any case he's silent for a while. But then he starts in again with the questioning.

—"Dear little princess," he writes?

—No, "Lilly,"

—Just "Lilly"?

—Maxi isn't his son.

Bald-Head glances at Maxi, who's fallen asleep in the back seat.

—He doesn't look like it, with that gloomy old-man face of his.

They converse for a while, and Bald-Head seems in a good mood. He questions her and marvels at her answers. He applauds the little princess who's set out so bravely on a journey to her father, just like in a fairy tale. Night falls around them. At the rest stop he says abruptly:

—Now I'll turn this cheeky little liar right over to the police, so that she'll get back to her parents. I'm sure they're already worried.

He catches her in a firm grip and pulls her behind him to the telephone booth. When he lets go a moment to open the door, she wriggles free and runs away.

SOME YOUNG PEOPLE take her along in their old VW bus over the Spanish border and to the ocean, then pay no further attention to her. Nor do they ask where she comes from and why she wants to go to Madrid. On the empty beach they had looked for a campsite for the night, then in the morning, with the first sunlight, they run naked in the waves. Lilly remains sitting in the car, where she spent the whole night in the backseat. Maxi is on the floor. She tied a cord around his foot, the end of which she keeps in her hand, so that he doesn't get up unnoticed while she's asleep and run away.

—So you can't swim?

A short fat boy huffs and puffs his way out of the water and throws himself onto a towel next to the VW bus. Lilly doesn't want to go in the water because of Maxi. Above all, she doesn't want to stay at this beach.

—You guys said you were driving to Madrid!

—That black-haired guy taking care of the bus says the

motor is broken. He says he'll get it back up though. He's a mechanic.

—When?

At this, however, he makes no move to check the motor. He gets a soccer ball out of the trunk and begins to kick it around.

—We'll see. Maybe tomorrow.

The car can't be broken. He's lying. Lilly picks a fight with him. She won't stand for his stupid tricks.

—Are you a Turk?

—So what if I am? he asks back, blinking in the sunlight.

—They slaughter animals, says Lilly.

—Everyone does.

—But not like *that*!

The Turkish boy grins at her.

—They just twitch a little, and then the blood runs out.

—Have you seen it?

Now he puts his dark face very close to hers, rolls his eyes, and lets his long tongue hang out.

—Dumbass!

Why is the fat boy staring at her so intently? What's his deal?

—You have braces like a girl! she says snippily.

—Boys have them too.

She's never seen a boy with braces before. Boys with braces probably live somewhere else.

—They must have cost a thousand euro!

—Way more!

—Your parents must be rich, if they cost so much.

—They're already dead, the boy declares, leaving his mouth open so Lilly can marvel at his braces.

—I think that's good.

—I think it's good that they're dead too, the boy says airily. I have the urn at home.

54

—Really?

—Well I can't just carry them all over!

—So you always get to do whatever you want?

—Yeah, of course.

—And what are you doing now?

—A world tour, first off.

—It could very well be, says Lilly with a grim countenance, that my Mama will be dead soon too.

—And your old man?

She doesn't answer. She doesn't want to say that he's the king of Spain, she doesn't want to make the boy jealous. And a world tour, only a boy could think that up. Where do you begin, and what's the destination, once you start traveling?

—So what does your world tour cost?

—I don't know yet, says the boy as if it doesn't matter, but since she looks at him severely, demanding an answer, he adds quickly: one million.

She's caught him out: it's all a lie to impress her, she knew it from the beginning.

—Your parents aren't even dead, you just ran away.

She stands up quickly to take away a little stone that Maxi has picked out of the grass and is trying to stick in his mouth.

—I don't have time to just hang around like you guys, I have a goal.

WHAT MAKES LIFE WORTH LIVING? Sebi: Hearing that school has burned down. Paula: Freshly squeezed carrot juice. Till: Caressing Anna and seeing in her face that she likes it. Susanne: My new jogging shoes. Sven: Watching myself slowly losing control. Holger: High heels. Christof: Snowflakes on Maren's eyelashes. Jerry Ann: Sleeping in Kevin's sweater. Flori: Getting lost in the woods and then finding my way again. Petra: Being in terrible danger, and then waking up and realizing it was only a dream. Dagmar: Going to medical school, finally. Iris: Having a visitor who just suddenly rings the doorbell and is there. Karli: Burning my old soccer jersey. Shirin: Going to the wrong party, but then finding that everyone's glad to see me anyway. Jens: Sex. Martin: I'd like to go to a country where there's a war. Ali: I want the Titanic not to have sunk. Uwe: Coming around the corner just when my worst enemy slips on a banana peel. Renate: Eating ice cream with Johnny Depp. Kim: I don't care! Fini: Hunting for mushrooms and finding some. Maren: Spelunkers. Paul: Winning the jackpot. Alice: Having someone scared of me. Frank: Swimming naked. Kathi: Being missed by friends. Claudia: Falling head over heels in and then probably out of love with Sascha. Martin: Life ain't easy for a boy named Sue. Alex: GOOOAAAAL! Bernd: Finally being able to really live. Oleg: Pfälzer liverwurst. Moritz: Boycotting the USA for the following reasons. Esther: Opening the window so a fly can escape. Florian: Hopping freight trains. Leon: Coming up with good excuses.

 —Found Object

ONCE I SAW A DEAD BOY, sitting on the pavement. I know you, I said to him, you're the boy who jumped down from the building up there! Then he laughed. He just laughed.

 —And you?

 —I ran away, says Lilly.

PEOPLE WILL LONG REMEMBER the housewarming party that Lisa gave in Dagmar's apartment, and not just because of its horrific ending, which naturally gave rise to wild speculation that could be neither disproven nor confirmed. Police investigations, too, remain inconclusive.

There's a veritable throng in the chic apartment. Many older, successful people from the cultural scene mingle with young people who are trying to network or who simply want to be in the thick of things. Lisa has invited almost everyone she knows, even her mother, although of course she didn't suppose Vanessa would attend the event, particularly since Lisa's exit from the garret, though temporary, was taken amiss. So how many people do you actually know, Lisa? An old man, bedecked with a red polka-dot bowtie, says: One day I'll write the name of every person I know, have known, and who is still alive in my head on the wall of my room. Not just long-dead uncles and aunts, not just childhood friends, old friends from the editorial office, or travel acquaintances, but also people whose names I've forgotten, or whose names I never knew. People I don't want to remember but who stubbornly inhabit my memory. The woman in the heavy winter sweater who squatted on some rubble on a sultry summer day and talked to herself... an alcoholic probably. During the two hours I spent at the café across the street I thought, I have to go and help the desperate creature, but I never did. Maybe that's why she's stayed so alive in my mind. And others, many others. How many are there, a thousand? Two thousand? More? How many would you guess?

—And that's not even counting the people we know from books, Albrecht intrudes. Madame Bovary and Furst Myshkin seem very alive to us.

—And Bugs Bunny! cries one of Lisa's girlfriends, who wants to spread good cheer, and is in fact rewarded with general laughter. She'd love to play guitar and sing one of her songs, but the room is too crowded. There's nowhere to sit, and the guests stand closely packed, with barely enough room to hold their soup cups and baguettes. A lucky pair is encamped on the bed where the coats have been discarded. There's goulash and there's wine, red and white, the cheap kind. With so many guests Lisa can't afford better. Mallmöh contributed a few bottles of champagne, which were quickly drunk. It's not necessary to entice them with fancy foods. The guests, even those used to gourmet restaurants—the wine connoisseurs and dessert lovers—accept simplicity here. It has, in fact, a certain allure, since it reminds them of the parties of their younger days, when they were all still students, when they were all bold and idealistic, when they disdained and derided the luxurious life. Now they joke about it, ironic and sentimental.

But one can't endure such a crowd long after midnight, or, as was once the case, till dawn. By twelve, nearly all the guests are gone. There's a clear view over the devastation in the two rooms and in the little kitchen, where sliced baguettes lie in puddles of coffee and the goulash sticks on the sides of the bowls. The refrigerator door hangs open.

—There's dessert! calls Lisa as she slides bowls of semolina pudding onto a tray.

—Who's still here?

Only Bonsack is still in the room. To free himself from the clamorous impositions of the party, he'd hastily torn the wrapping paper from the CD he brought for Lisa. Now, sunk deep in the chair, head thrown back and eyes closed, he listens to the music.

—Ha! "In a Glasshouse!" *Wesendonck*!

Bonsack looks dozily at the outstretched finger in front of his face. Albrecht has come back again and is trying to provoke the conversation that's been brewing all night.

—If only I had known you were a Wagnerian! Had I known earlier, you'd not have gotten off so easily!

For a while, like Bonsack, he listens to the song, but he can't keep quiet long:

58

—Oh, that's right! You published that totally Positivistic essay on D'Annuzio's Vittoriale! That makes sense! Now I can see the connection!

What does this burdensome man want? Ah yes, he's the unpleasant sort of person that tries to make himself interesting with sudden confrontations. Should I answer him? Tell him off with some suave irony? Even that would show too much respect for the brute! A long, astonished look at the blowhard will suffice. And now Lisa is back again, she grasps the delicate situation immediately, links arms with Albrecht and pulls him playfully away, laughing.

—No, no, not this subject, please! I have to send you home, pronto!

—But not him? Albrecht suppresses his anger with difficulty.

—Him too! Him too! she laughs brilliantly with her pretty predator's mouth, pushes the antagonist out the door, and returns to Bonsack, saying:

—You really have to go now too. I'm horribly tired.

—Just listen!

Bonsack stretches his arm out, eyes closed, searching for her. She wants to sidestep his hand, but doesn't dare leave the room and break the mood. She cowers in front of Bonsack on the carpet.

—Lisa!

She doesn't answer.

Bonsack acts surprised.

—Ah, there you are! I thought...no, I didn't really.

She holds his searching hand tight, and they listen to the music.

An abrasive sound startles them. Someone is hitting the glass of the patio door with a metal object. Albrecht's sweaty face, he won't stop hitting the pane with his flashlight. Stop,

stop! Three faces swarm behind the glass. Your young friends, Lisa! Two cheeky fellows next to Albrecht make faces, grin, open their eyes wide in pretend fright. Quit it with the pranks! Knock, knock, knock. The pane will break!

They're gone! Disappeared into the darkness of the front yard. Lisa stands up and gives the curtain an energetic tug across the night-darkened panes.

Bonsack concentrates on the song again and traces the music with a soft gesture. Interesting, he says as the CD ends and Lisa tries to invite him to go, I've never been to the Prado. Although I love Zuloaga so, and Coello too, of course...and Patinir....

Lisa gathers the ashtrays and calls from the kitchen:

—Albrecht knows Spanish!

—Ah, says Bonsack, and slowly straightens himself in the deep chair. You think I could do something for Albrecht. Yes, of course that's what she thought, she wanted to bring it up with her "he knows Spanish."

—That's not what I said.

The scornful grin pulls his mouth a bit crooked. It makes him ugly, Lisa thinks. She gets excited:

—He's already finished two novels. I typed them on the PC. We work together on them really. Are you listening? He wants me to make some serious revisions. He doesn't work like other people, above all he wants to hear his writing, so he speaks it aloud, records it on a tape, listens to it, erases some parts, makes cuts, and then I get the tape. It's hard for me sometimes. Words that he invents, or words that he changes, mangles, he just says them....

—For heaven's sake!

—It's hard for me to write those words. For example, on one of the tapes there's just a noise, like a kind of buzzing. What letters am I supposed to use for that? I look at the keys and have to choose

60

which letters... I criticize him sometimes, too, when I don't like something. (At this he raises his eyebrows.) I'm very critical!

—Oh really?

That sounds like mockery. (Why won't he take me seriously!)

—Neither of them has been published yet. And he's working on the third.

—It's amazing that he keeps going!

(He has no choice. But I stand by him.)

—Don't be so unfeeling. Put yourself in his place.

—I find that difficult.

(The false laugh again, the crooked mouth. Should I tell him how ugly it makes him look?)

—I can always put myself in someone else's place.

—In mine too?

(Scorn, always scorn.)

—But you could recommend him...somewhere...to a publisher...You have influence.

—Oh, you know....

(He's trying to blow me off. Egoist! I won't give up, though.)

—Do it!

—Ah, the publishing industry! (And now the arrogant guy starts right in with the complaining.) I don't know if one could even expect that much of him.

—Oh please, please! (I'm getting childish now, but he likes it when I act like a child.) Albrecht is definitely talented! (He can't resist, he's waking up again!)

—You know, says Bonsack, there have to be people, talented people, who remain unnoticed. Throughout their lives, never stepping into the limelight. That's the true cultural richness of a society. Undiscovered treasure, untainted by the marketplace.

(Shot down. Whatever you do, don't get offended! Act understanding.)

—I see.

—Think about it.

(You're just jealous, I can see that! But I'll get him on the subject of travel.)

—Oh, I'd love to go to Spain sometime. (He ignores this. Typical.)

—Anna never wants to come. (I was talking about myself, not Anna.) I don't know why she doesn't want to come. And alone...you know me. (Oh yes, I know you!) I need other people.... It's my puritanism, you know. (Yes, I know.) I really can't treat myself to anything special, anything beautiful, all alone. (Hypocrite!) I need someone to whom I can give it as a gift. Or at least that's what I have to tell myself.

(Just you wait, now I'm going to confront you about Dagmar!)

—You know, you pissed me off the other day.

—When?

—At the art opening.

—What happened?

(Pompous ass, as if you don't know!)

—Ah, you mean Dagmar!

(He pretends that it surprises him.)

—Your friend Dagmar? Who lets you live here? Are you jealous of your friend?

(No, no, no, three times no!)

—That would be a glimmer of hope, anyway.

Lisa has to defend herself against such suspicion!

—Jealous of Dagmar? No! I admire her, I just find her so beautiful! With her I could even...if she had a boyfriend, we could share.

—So why are you mad?

—Because of Anna. You flirt with Dagmar, and Anna stands next to you suffering, I've seen it. (I'm an excellent observer!)

Angrily she scoops up the glasses. One falls over and the leftover red wine drips on the carpet.

—Just leave the glasses!

—Who else is going to clean up?

—Women are always so capable, Bonsack whines coquettishly. Anna is always so capable! (His mouth is crooked again!) I always have capable women around me. Actually, I love quite the opposite...but you know that. (Yes, I know it, I know it.) I find a certain weakness erotic. It must be terrible for Anna, living with me.

—You have everything. (The interesting university job, the rich wife, you know interesting people...who else has that kind of luck!)

—*She* has everything! She has the house and the lake and the garden and the horse and the yew hedges and the swimming pool and the Art Deco furniture and even the paintings, although I'm the art historian. *She* has all that!

(Am I supposed to feel sorry for him? Soon he'll be envying me for having nothing.)

—You live in paradise.

—I'm a stranger in this paradise, I walk through it like a stranger...I stand by the pool...a stranger. But the worst part is this: I can't live without it. I need luxury! But it corrupts me, too. I'm a delicate person, I admit it. I love the beautiful, the brilliant. Bad taste pains me, you understand?... I'm dependent. And the worst of the worst: I resent Anna a bit for making this life possible for me. I don't want to be thankful, you understand? I'm sure you don't understand, Lisa. You don't know it, but you're lucky, you see everything so simply.

—I like living in this chic apartment, even though it's not mine. I'm enjoying these two months.

Bonsack sinks deep in the pillows. He gives her a long look and says:

—Let me stay here! I love you!

(That tone of his, I still recognize it!)

—Ah, this again?

—Yes, still and again.

(Your professions have really driven out the last vestiges of my affection.)

—It's too stressful, my love. I'll call you a taxi.

Where is the telephone? Slipped under the sofa, she fishes for it with her foot. The taxi number is continually busy.

Bonsack springs up quickly, throws on his jacket and is suddenly quite energetic, his erotic mood seems to have disappeared. (As if it just clicked off! He's not even cross anymore. Actually, I should be offended!)

—The taxi stand is on the corner. If there are none there, I'll come back.

—But only to use the phone, Lisa laughs, she's relieved. (I handled that quite well.)

And when Bonsack is gone, she cleans up, loads the glasses in the dishwasher, finds some leftover bits of food here and there that will have to be thrown away. The guests weren't exactly careful with things. A drop of red wine on the sofa, oh God! I'll try a little salt. And as she goes about, Lisa begins to undress. She takes the clip out, so that her long black hair falls free, takes her skirt off, slips her shoes off while standing up, almost falls over, hobbles in her hurry to roll down her stockings. A quick hop in the shower! Very hot, very cold, then hot again. The doorbell rings. He's back again after all! Of course he could have found a taxi, there are always some there, all night. He could have waited a bit until one came. How late is it? It's ringing again. Wait, just wait a sec! I'm in the shower! (I'm not going to be taken in by his sweet talk, in any case.) Shakes the hair from her face. Just a sec, yeah, a sec! Get the towel quickly. I can't go to the door naked. And I already locked up, just a sec, you hear? Where did I put the key? I have to look, have to look. Should I tell him I lost the key? The big towel falls from her shoulder, she has to knot it tight, it's so big. Wait, now I can open up.

Then, the last few things she perceives: the door thrusts open, catching her painfully on the elbow, something pushes her back, something tears her towel off, she wants to duck, but something holds her head clenched, three, four quick flashes, she sees a flash of something silver, and somewhere warmth wells out of her naked body. She opens her mouth to scream, but she can't make a sound. The shower is still running, like an idiot I didn't turn it off. I want to roll over, roll over, but I can't. Won't someone turn it off? I can't! I'll have to let the shower run until Dagmar's apartment overflows with red water.

ATTEMPT NUMBER TWO AT ALEIJADINHO. Aleijadinho, pious artist!

The dark-cloaked figure melts away from the stone angel, turns around.

In the too-bright light that falls in through the hastily opened door, the viceroy stands with his bizarre followers, exhausted and hot from the long climb, fanning themselves. On the flabby cheeks of the two white-powdered ladies, eye makeup runs like black tears.

—Your beautiful angel, Aleijadinho! How expressive the gesture of the hands is! How big the hands are! All your figures have such big, expressive hands, probably because you have none, Aleijadinho.

The giant cloaked figure moves now: Two figures are hidden beneath the sackcloth, one sits on the shoulders of the other. The wrapped stumps of two legs stick out like tree boughs, black and wizened. Aleijadinho now slips down surprisingly nimbly and squats, a wounded, lame-winged bird, helpless upon the stones. Near the dark bundle, his black slave looms like a giant.

—How many hands and feet and ecstatic faces are you going to knock out of this stone, little cripple?

—I can't count them on my fingers, sir!

At this he thrusts his tool-bound stumps angrily through his sleeves.

—So, little cripple, you think you're just not going to die?

The viceroy bends low to Aleijadinho in order to speak right in his face, and everyone bends down with him. In so doing, a strand of precious pearls falls from the towering wig of one of the continually giggling, cooing, gaudily befrilled mulatto ladies. The strand breaks, the pearls skip and clack over the tiles. Aleijadinho scoots nimbly after them, over here, over there, over the stone tiles, he sweeps them together with his sleeves, tries to catch the rolling, springing balls with the mallet and chisel on the stumps of his arms, bends far forward and snatches two or three...the fat lady screeches: With his mouth! What? He caught it with his mouth! Who? The little cripple! He swallowed it! Swallowed it down! You don't need to open your putrid little mouth, we certainly don't want to look in! But if tomorrow your ass spits out precious little pearls, then we'll all gather and watch!

HOW COULD YOU THINK that your father lives here?

—I saw him myself.

First she'd heard a hundred clattering heels on the marble tiles, she believes, and then suddenly she'd seen her father, seen how he'd come down the stairs with his whole retinue in quick mincing steps, hurried through the gallery and disappeared through the gate that opened silently before him.

Perfectly ordered stone masses in the sun-baked wasteland. Here the gout-ridden old king had locked himself up and ruled over an empire on which the sun never set. Here, in constant prayer, he had implored God's grace for his strict Catholic reign.

—They kneel there piously, hands folded, the king with the queen, his fourth wife. Behind him is the third, and, far in the background, the first, next to the unlucky Carlos. The artist made them so lifelike, Bonsack explains, that one could imagine the shining gold statues finishing their devotions, getting up, and walking away.

—Three women and one king! Dagmar laughs.

Bonsack has been leading Anna and Dagmar through the endless rooms of the Escorial for hours. All the paintings and frescoes, the sculptures, the furniture, and the altars give him the opportunity to show off his brilliance and knowledge. As always, Anna tries very hard, she prepared herself diligently, but what she adds here and there in the way of supplementary clarification he finds uninspired and lacking in deep understanding. The things don't speak to her. Dagmar's naive questions interest him more. They tempt him into giving long lectures wherein he grandly displays his preeminence. It amuses him that when he catches her out, she tries to hide her ignorance.

—So where is Albrecht hiding, our chaotic fellow traveler?

—He's flitted off somewhere, off track.

They've arranged to meet Albrecht at four in the entrance hall. But please, no later! There's no café, there's not even a place to sit. Gradually they've all grown ill-tempered, and they stand in the entrance hall watching the tourists as they swarm, alone or in clusters. How ugly they are! How unaesthetically they dress! The older and homelier they are, the greater exhibitionists! Instead of covering their withered flesh and fat bellies, they go about in shorts and let their flabby upper arms ooze out of undershirts.

—There's nothing less erotic to me than women's aging skin, says Bonsack. He flips hastily through the illustrated book that Anna has pressed in his hand. It almost disgusts me. He looks at both his companions, from Anna to Dagmar.

—I realize, naturally, that it's really quite immoral, sexist, yes, yes, but it has nothing to do with intelligence or reason... it's completely unconsidered, physical.

—You put up with that? Dagmar retorts so fiercely that it frightens Anna. Then she forces herself to smile. Dagmar, with yet more agitation:

—He means you, you know!

And before Anna can answer—probably to excuse his boorishness—Bonsack says with a laugh:

—Yes, of course I mean Anna! That's why she's smiling. I always mean Anna! She smiles at me! Haven't you noticed that yet?

Anna tries to take his shamelessness lightly.

—Adam, you're really overdoing it!

Dagmar impatiently interrupts the squabble:

—Where's Albrecht? It's almost half past!

Bonsack pointedly:

—Do you miss him?

He won't drop the subject. I love her, my Anna, that is to say, actually I love her more and more, when I think about it. I couldn't live without Anna, it would be completely, utterly impossible! And the more I love her, the less attractive I find her.

Anna's sad, smiling face.

—You put up with that, Anna?

If she won't answer, won't defend herself, won't run away, run away forever, then I'll continue this.

—So you mean that eroticism diminishes in proportion to

the increase of love?

—Precisely, Dagmar!

Anna already has the matches ready as he pats his pocket to find the cigarette case. Very classy, Bakelite, two-tone, Art Deco...clearly a gift from Anna for the three cigarettes per day that she allows him.

—It pains me, it makes me sad. Anna says it doesn't bother her.

Anna smiles, holds the burning match up for him. He takes it from her, he won't let her serve him.

—It actually pains me physically. The pains in my arms all come from that...these physical pains, sometimes all over... Good thing Albrecht's not here yet, he adds maliciously, now he'd ask: Are you happy? It's so nice to be with you two, without that insensitive interrogator. Why did we even bring him with us, do you remember why?

—He just forced his way in.

—We could have defended ourselves, though! Unfortunately we're not coarse enough.

—Look over there! The little girl scuttling away with the painting!

Now a school class jostles in, the child with her painting gets no farther. She gets stuck in the whirl of floundering arms and legs and flying pigtails, the rubble and hubbub. Holding the painting like a shield, she tries to channel her way to the exit. A boy falls over, another hits his head on the frame and begins to bawl. A teacher calls for security, the man comes running and holds the child with the painting tight. No, she won't give up the painting. A skirmish ensues, the security guard has her scrawny bare arm in his grip and she's forced to let go of the painting.

—She wanted to steal it! says Anna. Stupid child!

Bonsack is uninterested by the disturbance.

—It comforts me somewhat that Anna isn't hurt by the slights that I'm forced to inflict on her. He reaches and stretches his back, stubs the half-smoked cigarette out in a torn piece of foil.

—You have to be healthy enough to be able to repress everything!

—One can't repress everything, Dagmar counters energetically. She feels at home when the conversation turns to psychology. I believe, for example, that when one has a child, one has very simple, strong feelings. (Why did I think of children?)

—Too bad you don't want one, he says with a quick look away over his glasses. Dagmar laughs.

—Did I say that?

—And now Anna is too old.

The painful smile stays on Anna's face as she tries to broach another subject.

—You really have to read that little book by Machado, Adam! I'm almost finished with it.

—Unfortunately I really can't read at the moment. It's a dreadful state.

—He wants to lie in the dark, says Anna. So naturally I turn off the light.

—Yes, I lie in the dark and stare at the blinking light in the window. Across the street a green display goes on and off and on again, constantly. Sleep is out of the question!

Anna sighs sympathetically.

—The pulsing light, bright-dark-bright. I stare over and feel life trickling away. This night, another day. And nothing remains. Will I leave a trace? An oeuvre?

—Don't worry so much!

Anna wants to put her arm around him, but he fends her off.

70

—"Life's fleeting moment of happiness."

—What do you mean, Dagmar?

—That's what you wrote on the card with the lovely Watteau painting.

—"Pierrot content." Did I send that to you?

—No. You sent it to Lisa. The card is stuck in the bathroom mirror, it caught my eye immediately when they brought me back to the shambles of my apartment.

—Now I remember what I wrote: "In front of the dark wall, the five people, light like colorful moths, dust that one blows away. Pierrot content. Pierrot is happy. Life's fleeting moment of happiness."

—Lovely, Anna says.

—That painting always made me very sad. I thought, Bonsack says, that I had written that to Dagmar.

This is too much, Anna must get revenge.

—I admire you, Dagmar, she says with the most endearing smile, that you can still live in an apartment where such a dreadful thing happened! I could never do that! I thought Lisa was your best friend.

Dagmar doesn't answer. She says:

—Lisa had nothing personal in the apartment. Only a few clothes, a little makeup, nothing else.

—I couldn't do it, Anna insists. I wouldn't have a moment's peace, I'd always be thinking that the murderer had meant to get *me*.

—I do think that.

—You are so strong, Dagmar.

Bonsack looks reflectively at the two women.

—I don't find a single trace of Lisa in my feelings. Curious.... No matter how hard I search!

HABLA ALGIEN ALEMÁN Y ESPAÑOL?

Yes, Albrecht knows Spanish. He volunteers to act as translator in the preliminary interrogation of the little German thief. They sit in a windowless room with dark walls, which seems to be used as an office. Lilly nearly disappears in the old armchair, and the policeman has taken a seat behind the empty desk. Albrecht sits on a stool that has been fetched for him. No, he'd rather stand. He chastises the tourists that crowd through the open door with a look of hatred. Where are you from? She names a place that no one has ever heard of, maybe she made it up. In Germany? Yes, in Germany. Why did you come to Spain? Lilly doesn't answer. Why did you steal the painting? The King's in it, she says without looking up. Who asked you to do it? No one. Did you want to sell the painting? I don't want to, she answers defiantly, as if it were rightfully hers. Do you know what a painting like that costs? I don't know. But she thinks it must be very expensive, since the King is painted on it. When Albrecht presses her, she doesn't answer, or she lowers her head defiantly. This makes the police officer furious. What are we going to do with this arrogant German beast? She should at least stand up when she answers. The tourists in the doorway are not satisfied with the progress of the interrogation. They should really be able to manage a little girl! A woman swats at Lilly with her handbag, causing the clasp to open and a few objects to clatter to the stone floor.

—Leave the child in peace!

Albrecht is irritated. The woman looks at him angrily:

—And who are you?

Should I explain to her why I've traveled here with my friends? Should I tell her what I strive for in everything that I do? To be closer to life, that's what I want. To plunge down into the roaring stream of events and bring up a piece of gold from the deep and show it to everyone, to shame you all! You, all of

72

you so nicely ensconced in your false lives!

And with sudden insight he says cheerfully what he has never said before:

—I'm an author. I write.

This hardly gratifies the woman, however. She rummages in her handbag to ensure that nothing has been stolen, and grumbles so loudly that everyone can hear.

—Then you should write: "A child who steals is a disgrace to Germany." And underline it three times!

A magnificent realization comes to him, more thrilling than the hunks of canvas on the walls, the whole dreary religious shebang in the imperial rooms that he roamed through in the misguided hope of finding something interesting: It's all lifeless! Art is so superfluous! I'd have nothing against throwing it all in a pile and letting it go up in flames. How Bonsack in his vanity pronounces the names with such pleasure, he positively lets them melt on his tongue: Velázquez, El Greco.... I feel distaste just hearing that silky, refined tone of voice. Why did I even come? The Escorial! I should have declined the offer! One gets pressured, hesitates out of indifference, is probably even flattered, and then suddenly it's too late to say no. Lisa always wants to get me together with Bonsack. He could be so important for me, for my "discovery," as she calls it. I'll tell you why this absurd trip has a point for me, Lisa. I know now. I didn't know before, but I know now. I came because of the little thief. You won't believe it, it isn't even logical, I had no idea of her existence. I have to talk to her again alone, I need to take notes. Bonsack and his women are already long gone anyway. It's after five.

—Let me talk to her one more time, *Señores*. I think I can get out of her who put her up to the theft, whether she's part of a gang or whether she came up with the crazy idea to take the painting off the wall on her own. She wouldn't have gotten far with her prize anyway.

They've locked Lilly in a small room, but they'll let her go when everything is resolved. What could they do with her, anyway? The embassy will be notified. She squats on the floor with an angry look on her face. Two nuns have taken Maxi away to be washed.

—Tell me something. How you live, what you do, who your friends are.

With three fingers Albrecht tries to turn the little girl's averted head toward him, but she shakes herself free.

—You don't need to tell me lies, just tell me how it is.

—Nothing special. I'm totally normal.

—Normal! Albrecht cheers, I'm going to write that down. She rebukes him angrily:

—You are *not* going to write that down!

He's warmed up now, hungry for a conversation.

—Look, I have a little red notebook here, I always keep it with me. And when I encounter something special or when I have an interesting thought, I make a note of it.

But he's still speaking of himself, that he's an author, why he writes, why he wants to make a note of what he finds significant. Does that interest the little thief? He pauses and looks at her searchingly.

—When I see something special, I write it down. But what is special? It's my subjective view that makes it special.

The little girl doesn't get it, of course. She snarls, without looking at him:

—What do you want from me, anyway?

—Good question!

—I asked what you want from me!

—I'm studying you right now, you asocial little fly. And he looks for her eyes, her gaze.

—Here's a photo of me.

She takes it quickly out of her bag and holds it up to Albrecht, without lifting her head. Albrecht examines the crumpled, dirty picture, and gives it back to her, disappointed.

—You're not in there at all.

Why did she give me the picture? What am I supposed to do with it?

—All I see in this picture is a deer, and it's jumping away, it's nearly disappeared.

—Yes, says Lilly, pinching her mouth together. It jumped away.

—Did you take the picture yourself?

—And you're from the police, Lilly accuses with a hurt look.

—No, no, quite the opposite! I'm an author.

—Whatever. And after a pause: What is that?

—Good question! Brilliant! Stunning! You're a star, kid! You have no idea how deeply that innocent question moves me.

—I don't care.

—An author is...an author...that's a really fundamental question. When he's published a book, then a person can claim to be an author. But if no one, if not one person has read the book, am I an author?

—I don't care.

—You've probably never read a book.

—I don't need to.

—Marvelous! I'll tell Bonsack that! I can turn that into something that will drive him crazy!

WHEN THE STRANGELY CONTORTED BODY was discovered hanging from the power line, everyone puzzled over what it could be: a windsock, a kite that had gotten caught on the wire, a doll, or a human body. They puzzled too, once they discovered that it was indeed a human body, over how the accident could have occurred. Had the man climbed up there to do some repairs? Or was he a suicide, who had chosen a remarkable way to kill himself, high above everything, between heaven and earth? And did he not look, when seen from the parking lot below, did he not look like he was crucified, like some terrifying omen in the drizzly gray of dawn? There was no lack of conjecture, but even the newspaper reports of the following days remained speculative. The dead man had come from Hannover, with unclear intentions. He seemed to have led a normal middle-class existence. Lawyer, well-salaried, stable family. His wife declined to give more specific information, and the son was away on a trip. In the dead man's charred jacket, the police found a piece of writing, now rendered illegible, which yielded no clues to his person. It was therefore assumed that it was in a fit of insanity that the man had chosen this bizarre, horrifying death.

IT'LL ALL BE BETTER NOW, Lilly. Believe me, now that you're back, everything will be better!

Lilly surveys her mother coldly. She's suddenly been seized with the desire to paint Lilly's fingernails red, and in the endeavor, drunk as she is, she's forgotten all other work. She wipes the wet strips of beet peelings off the table with the sleeve of her robe, but leaves them lying on the floor. She had almost slipped and fallen at the kitchen cupboard when she went to get the little bottle with the nail polish. She can't keep her balance anymore, and Lilly just watches and won't budge from her chair to help. Lilly's passive gaze angers her, giving her momentary strength and finally, with great effort, she manages to right herself. She shuffles herself onto the chair and holds Lilly's hand down violently on the damp and dirty

76

tabletop, splaying Lilly's fingers apart.

—Hold still...Lilly, don't pull your hand away, Lilly..., she mumbles in a gravelly voice, suddenly she's afraid that Lilly will rebel and run away. But Lilly doesn't defend herself, she lets everything be done to her. She sits stiffly, keeping distance between them, and looks at her mother, who keeps trying to toss her frizzy, sticky hair out of her face with a swift flick of her head, something she could once do quite elegantly. Now the strands just hang, and she sweeps them to the side with her hand, leaving red streaks on her forehead from the tiny paintbrush, which she still holds between thumb and pointer finger. She doesn't notice. Lilly looks at her mother and waits motionless until she attends to Lilly's fingernails again. She hears her mother's soft, nearly unintelligible babbling:

—It'll all be better, and you don't have to run away to Spain, Lilly. Now you'll stay here with me.

The mother throws Lilly a long look, full of expectation.

—...when I go back to work—they want me back, of course they want me back...

—Who does? Lilly demands severely.

—Anytime! I can start immediately. When I bus glasses from the tables, none of 'em get broken. Not a one! And from just tips alone...we'll put them in the green box, and you'll always get to count it. I'll buy myself a fur coat from Hirmer... Even if it's summer. Who cares! And I'll buy you something too. Lilly! Make a wish.

Lilly shakes her head energetically and for so long that her mother looks up from the nail brush.

—Why are you shaking your head now, you stupid hussy!

—There's nothing I want.

The slight makes her furious.

—You already have everything? And she wipes the wet table a few times with a sweeping gesture of her sleeve, as if to show who calls the shots in this kitchen. You already stole money from me out of the green box, Lilly. I heard clinking, and then all the cash was gone. But I didn't say a thing. I could've reported you, the police would've come for you!

Fritz appears with his aviator cap in the open window and asks with a smirk:

—What is this, a beauty parlor?

—Yes, screams the drunken woman, letting go of Lilly's hand, the manicure already forgotten. Yes! I'm going to be a beauty queen, I'm getting a facelift.

—You, ha...you...yeah right! jeers the man with the aviator cap.

The mother can't stand to be ridiculed by an ugly old man!

—He doesn't know shit about beauty! A sharp crease of anger begins to etch itself on Lilly's brow.

—I know all about it! It would last a day, then everything would slip right down again. Your face would slide down to the basement.

Lilly's mother stares at the man in shock, she plucks and tugs at her face and opens the trembling robe to show him her blotchy naked body.

—Look here...or there...the wrinkles...all gone...This is only from alcohol, it's just...I'm still young.

—Oh yeah, like you don't need to drink!

—I don't! I only drink because of you!

The man with the aviator cap forms his toothless mouth into a scornful: Ha! Ha!

The drunken woman runs to the window and screams at the man outside:

—You stay there! You're way too old for me anyway!

—Ha! He ducks under the windowsill, then runs away.

She has a hard time getting her slip and robe back in order, she gives up. She fishes for Lilly's hand and looks at her penitently: Do you hate me now? She still wants to finish polishing Lilly's nails, but shakes so violently that it becomes impossible. She slips with the brush and smears Lilly's whole finger with the sticky red color.

—Your other hand too! Give it here!

—I'd rather not.

—Oh God, oh God, you'd rather not! whimpers the mother. Give me your other hand, I'll put some pretty polish on that one too.

Lilly lays her other hand obediently on the tabletop, but tries to protest.

—It's all smeared!

—What's smeared?

As if Mother can't see for herself! Her mother shouts back:

—Oh for Christ's sake! It's not that bad! She sweeps the little bottle off the table. Let me see! Here, we'll wipe it off with a towel. No, what am I thinking...We'll use nail polish remover. Let me see! She pulls Lilly's hand fiercely toward her.

—Awful...awful, she whines. That looks awful, Lilly... Look, the brush is busted, it's all wobbly...And she presses the scraggly red bristles against the table. See, it's wobbly! Piece of shit!

She crushes the red brush against the table again and again, until no more red oozes out. Then she starts to cry, still staring at Lilly's red-smeared hand.

Lilly watches her, watches how she cries, soundlessly. She observes her calmly, without sympathy, without the slightest stir of emotion. It's quite still in the kitchen. Only a fly, a fat, shimmering green blowfly, buzzes around Lilly's face and crashes again and again against the windowpane.

Lilly commands her mother: Come now!

Now docile, she lets herself be helped up and led into the dark bedroom. Lilly has always entered this room reluctantly, she has a vague fear of its darkness, which even during the day is broken only by two tracks of light from tears in the blinds. The dust floats up and down, it swirls in chaotic waves as she comes in. The lamp on the nightstand no longer works. The glass bulb is shattered, probably from a fight. And that celluloid doll she'd once stepped on, how unpleasant that was! The cracking noise, the crushed head, the smooth pink body with its leg bent askew. The old geezer had brought it home one day and had given it not to Lilly, but instead to her mother, who didn't want it. There was a blowup and shouting, and finally he'd put it on the shelf, next to a plaster Lourdes Madonna that sat there gathering dust. It must have fallen down. Lilly used to imagine that it was not human bodies that lay among the pillows and mounded blankets, writhing around, but rather strange, shapeless animals, who cried or moaned now and then, as if they were being tormented. It never occurred to her that one of these beings could be her mother, despite the fact that she had often seen her mother enter the room. She transformed in the darkness of the room, perhaps. It smells like dog in there, Lilly thinks, it's smelled like dog since Fritz has been around. Lilly rushes back out, goes to the refrigerator, fetches two bottles of beer, then a third, and places them on the floor inside the half-open door without going into the dark room. Back to the refrigerator. She stabs at the button on the TV as she goes by. The plastic bag is ripped, she looks for another. The refrigerator door still hangs open, she cleans it out: sausage, shrink-wrapped cheese, two cartons of milk. She puts the apple juice back, since it's already been opened. Everything else gets dumped into the bag. The box of Nesquik, the oatmeal. She eyes a loaf of white bread, then tears the package open and tosses half the slices back in the fridge, along with a greasy tub of margarine. The music is getting louder. A clatter of horse hooves, a chase. A rocky red landscape. Where is Maxi? She calls to him.

—Maxi!

He's outside, standing next to the abandoned doghouse. She wants to beckon him in, then sees the old man standing outside near the window, so she pulls away and dashes across the room to the door. Loud male voices behind her, shots. The old man appears again, but then vanishes into the shed. The motor sputters and won't start. Lilly at the window. The moped is there, leaning quite calmly against the wall. Isn't he going to drive away? There's such a racket behind her! Lilly turns around, sees one man fall off his horse, then another, dead. For a moment she sees the old man smirking at her from the kitchen table. How did he get into the kitchen so suddenly? And the door is open, the door to the dark room, how did it creep open again? The moped outside begins to chug. The motor has finally started. The old man crouches on the bike...but he was just sitting behind her at the kitchen table with his scornful Ha! Ha! And now she sees him driving away, the straps of his cap fluttering around his head. Lilly takes Maxi's shirt and leggings from the drying rack. The huge rocky landscape again, she's glad not to be there! Lilly pockets some cookies, takes money from the green box in the cupboard, searches the man's coat on the rack near the door but finds nothing. The big bearded man stands in front of an abyss, screams:

—Come over!

—I dunno.

—Get a running start, Joe, then jump over!

—I dunno.

She finds a flashlight in a drawer. A hairbrush, a mirror, a few cassette tapes. Everything into the bag! The hammer is lying there too. Who put it there? She throws it on top of the stuffed bag, but it clatters to the floor.

The man's voice:

—I'm going to count to three...fine, I'll make an exception

and count to five, just to be nice.

—You don't need to count.

—I'm waiting.

She picks up the hammer and examines it. The price tag is still stuck on, she scratches it off. There's no more room—when she stuffs it in the pointy end gets caught on the clothing. Is the old man still in the dark room? Can't be, he already vroomed away on his bike. She holds the hammer in her hand and listens intently at the open door.

Suddenly the music breaks off and a male voice commands:

—Get a running start, and then jump over!

—Dumbass, Lilly curses. She forgot her yellow sweater, it might be freezing in Spain this time. She lays the hammer down on the table and fishes her sweater out of the dresser.

—How far of a jump is it?

—I didn't fucking measure while I was jumping, sorry.

—What?

—I said, "sorry!"

—She stuffs the sweater into the plastic bag with the shaft of the hammer. In the dark room, the strange animal has begun to move, it falls heavily down from a piece of furniture. It had better not creep out of its cave and start breathing fire!

The guy with the scar:

—Let me just light up another cig. After that!

She goes into the dark room but stays close by the door, listening into the silence. When nothing stirs, she says loudly and decisively:

—I'm leaving now.

When she receives no answer, only a faint rumbling, she says it again:

—I'm leaving now. I'm taking Maxi.

What is the animal doing? Lilly holds her breath and lurks, waiting to see if it will move. Vaguely she sees a formless mass pushing toward her, it becomes bigger and bigger until it completely fills the darkness. The huge dark animal wants to devour her. Fear grips her. She still has the hammer in her hand. She strikes, the hammer hits something hard. Something cracks. A gurgling sound. She strikes again. She sees frizzy hair, an eye amid the swollen flesh. She strikes again. The claw pierces deep, and the hammer gets stuck in the body.

The guy with the scar, his grin:

—What kind of a guy are you, huh? Are you an Eskimo? An amputated Yankee? Or what? A Chinese clown? Hey! You! And after a long silence:

—Run, man!

She won't get far with Maxi this time, they'll be looking for her: the police, the bureau of child welfare, the investigators. Curious eyes will find her eventually. Or perhaps she'll make her way through countries and continents untroubled, unmolested, and reach the great steps, where the prophets and martyrs of Aleijadinho are frozen in stone as if enchanted, immortalized in dramatic gestures and ecstatic poses. With a multitude of unknown others she climbs the steps. When the mist clears, scattered by the hot Brazilian sun, the whole shimmering heavenbound stairway becomes visible, swaying in a great arc through the immensity of the landscape. In the brightness above, the contours blur, the figures of the pilgrims dissolve in the light.

—And who are *you*? Lilly asks. She picks Maxi up from the step where she's laid him, for a moment, to rest. She wants to show him the head in the tattered black bundle that she nearly tripped over. Under the dark hood, eyes flit here and there. The gaping, lipless mouth rumbles and gasps, emitting inarticulate sounds. Look, Maxi! She bends down to the dirty bundle and stares into the wasted face:

—Man, you're really a sight!
And climbs onward, up the steps.

Translator's Afterword

In January 2012 I had the pleasure and honor of meeting celebrated German author Tankred Dorst and Ursula Ehler, his partner in writing and life, at their home in Munich. When I asked him when he began writing plays, his answer was "Always." When I foolishly questioned him about whether he was working on anything new, he responded, "Every day." These answers are a good introduction to the man and his work. In his late eighties, Dorst still tirelessly engages in new projects, works with new ideas, and explores new forms. With this tirelessness and willingness to explore comes an essential timeliness. As Georg Hensel remarked when Dorst received the 1990 Georg Büchner Prize, "For 30 years Dorst's plays have responded to the great transformations. He has always been a companion to the times."

Born in 1925, Tankred Dorst is best known as a playwright. His first major plays were produced in 1960 and have since enjoyed much success all over the world. Dorst's work is influenced by the theater of the absurd, but his monumental drama *Merlin, Or the Barren Land*, has also been compared to Goethe's *Faust* and is defiantly groundbreaking in its own right.

Despite its great importance and influence on German theater and letters, Dorst's work is still relatively unknown in America. *This Beautiful Place* is the first book in English totally devoted to a piece of his writing. This is particularly ironic and unfortunate, given the strong influence of American culture, not to mention the country itself, on both his writing and personal history. At the age of 17, Dorst was conscripted into the German army but was soon captured as a prisoner of war and sent to an internment camp on the Hudson River. Here, German POWs were put to work by the American military. Seeing the country for the first time had a great effect on the young Dorst, as, of course, did the strange experience of being "guarded" by American men his own age. He was at once introduced to the country and separated from it: by age he was a brother to the Americans, yet by nationality he was their prisoner. This mirroring effect—this parallel encounter with the "other"—is an important part of Dorst's work. It is also an aspect that makes translation of Dorst's writing thrilling and necessary: it is a chance to experience American culture through a German lens. Likewise, through the inescapable effects of translation, it is also a chance to see German culture through an American lens.

This Beautiful Place, Dorst's only novella, is notable in his oeuvre. Dorst has never been confined by strict genre rules and has worked in film, radio, and as a stage director (notably of Wagner's *Ring* cycle in Bayreuth in 2006), and the stamp of drama is ever-present in his work. *This Beautiful Place* was, in fact, first conceived as a screenplay, and work on the project in that form began long before the final prose incarnation took shape. The book is comprised of short episodes from the lives of several characters, stories which eventually intertwine. In this way, one can see the influence of episodic films such as *Short Cuts* and *Nashville* by the American director Robert Altman. Altman's style, with its emphasis on luck and fate, coupled with dark undercurrents of tragedy and dissatisfaction, had a strong effect not only on Dorst, but on German culture and writing from the last quarter of the twentieth century through to the present day. The dark and fragmented quality that Altman picks up on is the version of American culture that is most notably reflected in *This Beautiful Place*.

In Dorst's work we do not get a straightforward reflection, however: *This Beautiful Place* twists and bends the Altmanesque vision of society, with a result that is stranger, newer, and arguably darker than what inspired it. This is hardly surprising, in light of the fact that Dorst's initial firsthand encounter with

America came about through war, and his first viewing of the country was as a prisoner. The overt references to luck in *This Beautiful Place* are nearly always associated with anxiety and uncertainty. When Bonsack cries, "I demand my right to unhappiness. I'm in search of an abyss to hurl myself into," (p. 40) he could be writing an epigraph to the novella. Not coincidentally, the German word for happiness (*Glück*) is the same as the word for luck. When Aleijadinho refers to the luck he will need to complete the project that is his life's work (p. 41), one is struck by the sense that it is nothing more than luck—good or bad—upon which his life, his work, and indeed all meaning depend. Yet when all depends on luck, there is also room for hope. The tension between tragedy and hope, fantasy and reality, begins and ends the book and runs through it as one of its most important themes. In the striking opening scene, in which the two young lovers jump out a window to their deaths (p. 7), the horrifying act is immediately followed by a beautiful, peaceful image: "...then there's only the square of bright empty sky framed in the open window." Built within this image is the chance for hope: "there's only" gives the reader at least one moment to believe that the tragedy never actually occurred, that perhaps this moment of beauty is all there is.

The implicit question at the heart of *This Beautiful Place* and at the center of Dorst's writing in general asks: What happens when dreams are forced to confront reality? It is for Dorst an essentially political question; many of Dorst's major works, such as *Merlin* and *Toller*, depict the situation of an intellectual or idealist confronted with a concrete political or historical situation. But the oblique and surreal manner in which Dorst poses and explores this question in *This Beautiful Place* gives it dimensions beyond the political: it is a question of art and of humanity. The effects of this confrontation are, admittedly, often brutal, but the title of the book is and remains hopeful.

"*This Beautiful Place*" implies the persistence of these dreams, if not their ultimate triumph.

Lilly's journey to find her father is an excellent example of this confrontation between dreams and reality, and its brutality and hopefulness. The figure of the King of Spain is not a "real" character: we do not see his actions or hear him speak. Rather, he is the embodiment of this confrontation. The King of Spain is for Lilly a dream of what her life could be: magical, epic, worthy, and beautiful. To her, however, this dream is not mere fantasy, but reality. When she travels to Spain, she is bursting with the impending joy of meeting her true father, the King, and of finally being loved and respected. When she arrives, however, the curtain pulls back to display not the colorful, shining world she expected to see hiding behind her dull gray life of poverty and neglect, but rather the same harsh adult world that she has been prematurely forced to navigate (p. 69, pp. 72-75). Lilly's dream evaporates, leaving nothing more material than a painting, a two-dimensional representation of her fantasy, which she nonetheless clutches, unwilling to let it go. It is this continuing inability to distinguish what is real from what is imagined that leads to the brutal death of Lilly's mother (p. 83). But this is not the end for Lilly, or for the book. Instead, it ends with a dream, an alternate reality: "Or perhaps," we read, Lilly makes it to the mythical steps with Aleijadinho's finished creations. *Perhaps* she "climbs onward, up the steps."

In this maze of episodes, this haze of dreams, this difficult terrain of interior and exterior voices and intertwining narratives, what is there to fix on, to find as a thread? The dreaminess of the book lends itself to a sense of nihilism and groundlessness, but the guiding images of the book also work in the opposite direction. The opening scene perfectly embodies this tension between nihilism and affirmation of existence. When the old man who has witnessed the young couple's suicide converses with the boy's ghost, he finds the boy happy with his choice, but the section ends with the old man's comment, "[Dead is] no way to be, son, that is no way to be" (p. 9). These characters never return, but an essential theme has been established: That of perseverance, of striving towards beauty, and the idea of *being,* of survivingm as beautiful, in contrast to an oblivion that is pitted as its only opposite.

Dorst finds beauty in strange places, however—sometimes even in images of death and decay. The figure of Aleijadinho provides us with one of the central images of decay and beauty in the book. A legendary Brazilian sculptor (1738-1813) afflicted with leprosy, Aleijadinho embodies the holiness of striving towards beauty, as well as the contrast between soul and body. Dorst even skillfully adapts his narrative style in order to highlight this contrast, rendering the decaying body of the dying artist in some of the most lyrical, flowing prose of the book (p. 29).

The story of Aleijadinho also exemplifies another essential theme of the book: that of the tension between chaos and order. At the same time that the order of Aleijadinho's body decays into chaos, he is also turning nature's chaos into art's order by sculpting forms into the side of a mountain. "Why can't a ladder, as Jacob dreamed, reach to heaven?" asks a character earlier in the book (p. 30). The ladder, a miracle, is seen as a triumph of chaos over order. This tension between chaos and order is often a challenge to preserve in translation. As a translator, one is often tempted to make order from chaos: specifically from the "chaos" of a foreign language, a strange style, a fragmented structure. And to a certain extent, this is necessary—it is indeed the charge of the translator to wrangle words and sentences from one unruly language to another and to come up with a result that feels complete and beautiful. In another way, however, the best way to translate something that doesn't seem logical is on its own terms, and much of the strangeness of the story must be preserved, even on the linguistic level.

It is inherent to the meaning of dreams and fantasies that they lie forever slightly out of reach, that they are essentially materially ungraspable. This ungraspability is another of the challenges I encountered in translating this book, but it is a fortuitous struggle, as the striving towards something unreachable is essentially the work of this novella. This idea is present both in the original title, and in my English translation. The book's German title is *Der Schöne Ort*, which translates literally as *The* Beautiful Place, rather than *This*, as I have chosen to render it in English. The choice to substitute "this" for "the" has to do with the fact that "this" mimics a sort of pointing gesture of the German article "der" which "the" does not imply. "This" place at first seems a very concrete idea, but when examined closely it is more open, less certain than "the." It is "this" place that we have in our minds, "this" beautiful place that we long for but perhaps can barely describe, rather than "the" place of reality.

It was also a challenge to capture Dorst's idiosyncratic prose style. His playwriting background is clear in his prose writing, and the stage-direction-like partial sentences and lengthy inner monologues often proved difficult to render in English without seeming simply like fragments or run-ons. Here I chose to use commas to punctuate long sentences, even though this is unusual, even "incorrect," in English, rather than creating sentence fragments by using periods, because I feel that this style is essential to the flowing, stream-of-(un)consciousness quality of the original. Indeed, the book is not only *about* dreams, but also structured by a sort of dream-logic. It is filled with striking images that can best be understood simply as images from a dream or, at times, a nightmare.

The episodic construction was also difficult to replicate in English, since the prose style and mood changes with each episode. Tenses and perspectives shift quickly as interior and exterior monologues switch and overlap, and the translator must follow these strains of voice and thought like the voices in a fugue, making sure that each one stays distinct and can be heard clearly. It is also these strong mood and tone changes that make the book as exciting as an intricate fugue, or a play with frequent, elaborate set changes, and it is this which has been such a challenge and pleasure to capture. In the end, translating this work is not just a pleasure; it is a duty and an honor. I cannot think of a better way to encapsulate this duty than Dorst's own words:

...we don't know the future. I think it is up to us to devote all of the energies and the talents that have been given to us – by whom we do not know – to protect from this uncertain future our wicked, beautiful and imperfect present, our irrational dreams and fruitless exertions.

Anne Posten

91